The Lyons

Kay Snow

The Lyons Copyright © 2021 by Kay Snow. All Rights Reserved.

All rights reserved. Kay Snow asserts the moral rights to be identified as the author of this work. No part of this book may be reproduced in any form or by any electronic or mechanical means including information storage and retrieval systems, without permission in writing from the author. The only exception is by a reviewer, who may quote short excerpts in a review.

Cover designed by David Collins and Kay Snow

This book is a work of fiction. Names, characters, places, and incidents either are products of the author's imagination or are used fictitiously. Any resemblance to actual persons, living or dead, events, or locales is entirely coincidental.

Kay Snow
Visit my website at kaysnow.co.uk

Printed in Great Britain by Amazon

First Printing: December 2021

For my soulmate – I love you beyond words.

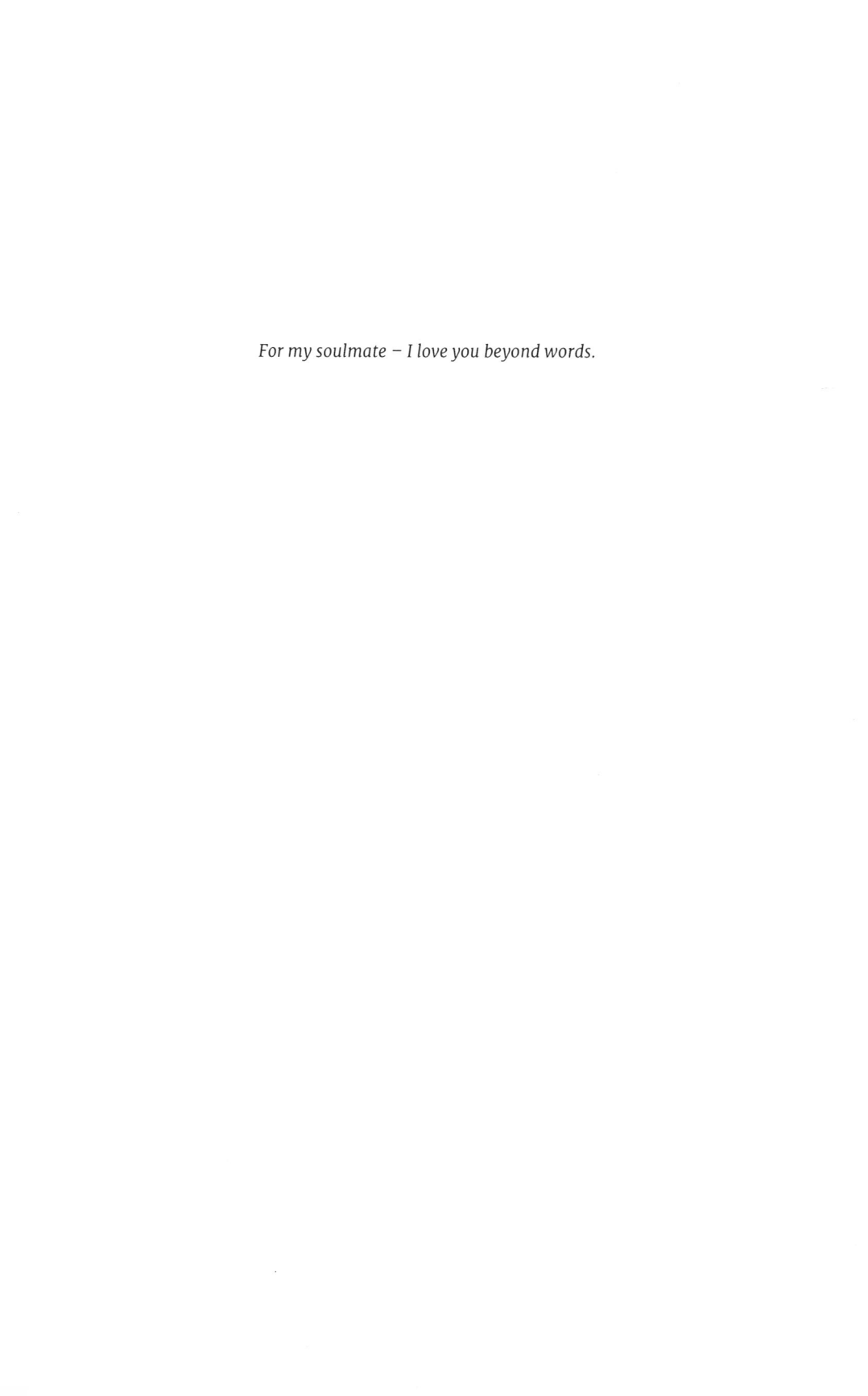

The distinction between past, present, and future is only a stubbornly persistent illusion.
—ALBERT EINSTEIN

Prologue

The pond's icy armour lay firm and strong, protecting its soft underbelly.

All but one slice remained, as if a portion had been taken out like a piece of pie. There, it was split into deathly sharp shards as if something, or someone, had broken through and disappeared beneath.

An icy scar already began its formation on the still trembling surface, busily knitting all the pieces back together, as if in eagerness to cover up a terrible misdeed.

The man sank beside the pond and sobbed so heartwrenchingly, the angels themselves looked down upon him with sadness, and cried...

Part One

Kathryn White

Chapter 1

t was a cold, but pleasant September afternoon as the white Range Rover indicated left onto Coach Road. Sat warmly within, was Kathryn White, and her sister Anna.

"That did say Coach Road, didn't it?"

"Yes," confirmed Anna. "I wish you'd get your eyes tested."

"My eyes are thirty-three years old; it's natural to struggle with reading distant signs," she laughed.

"It wasn't *miles* away. It was quite close. Anyway, you do as you please, you always do. Just like with this house."

"I wish you wouldn't worry so much. I haven't even seen the place yet. No doubt it'll be a pale comparison to the photographs in the sales brochure. They usually are, so I may not like it."

Anna twisted a piece of her short, auburn hair round her finger whilst casting her sister a knowing look. "I'm sure that you'll fall in love with it at first sight. You always love old things and bygone days. Don't get me wrong; I can find them enamouring too. But you, I'm sure that if you were plucked from this time and placed into the early 20th Century, you would accept it and no doubt relish in it."

"I would! I adore big old houses. It's soul-destroying when I think of all the lost country houses of England that've been left to ruin. Or worse still, destroyed. Fancy demolishing wonderful architecture that took months to design, and years to build. All those skilled craftspeople that spent millions of hours no doubt, carving complex designs from stone to create the finest buildings ever made. Fast forward a hundred years or so, and it's more important to make way for progress and knock them down. I wouldn't call a new motorway advancement, would you?"

"Yes. Yes, I would," laughed Anna.

"Oh, look. This *is* the right road; look there. Mrs Carter said to watch out for the gateposts to Lyon House." She stopped the car, got out, and walked gleefully up to them.

Two substantial gateposts, each featuring a prominent lion statue, marked the entrance of the road. The lions surveyed the area with an air of indifference, while Kathryn thoughtfully traced her fingers across the stone. The word 'Lyon' was inscribed on the left post, and 'House' was engraved on the right.

She thought in awed admiration of all the brilliant artisans who painstakingly chipped, and chiselled away to produce these beautiful works of art.

Both lions were laid dramatically, and though they appeared relaxed, she had an unexpected and strange sensation they were *most* aware of *all* who passed by these posts.

The lion to the left had his mighty paws crossed imperturbably, whilst the other licked his right paw clean.

She wondered how many people had done as she was doing now, and how many souls these superior creatures had seen come, and watched go from the house. She was genuinely mesmerised by them. And they, too, she thought chillingly, were mesmerised by her.

"Kathryn. Kathryn, come on. Your Mrs Carter will be waiting for us."

"I'm coming." She closed the car door gently and clicked the seatbelt into its place.

As they began the mile-long drive to Lyon House, the sun shone radiantly down and cavorted through the embrowned decorous chestnut tree-lined road, to then dance lightly upon its surface.

Kathryn breathed in deeply – she was excited. This was to be a new chapter in her life. The beginning of a dream come true.

She was unable to express her level of excitement to Anna, as it had been less than a year since their father's passing, and Anna remained deeply affected by the loss. As was she, but she had determined that their father would not want them to be corralled inside the large family home forever. He would want them to live their lives and consequent dreams.

He had left a substantial fortune in which each of them had a share. But Anna refused to live anywhere else. She said she 'felt close to Dad' whilst there.

Much to Kathryn's displeasure, Anna had developed an unhealthy fascination with the afterlife, which involved inviting numerous mediums and psychics to their residence in an attempt to contact their father. Naturally, these efforts proved unproductive, but Anna remained persistent.

She persuaded one of the psychics to instruct her on how to read tarot cards. Consequently, she never went anywhere without them and, to Kathryn's chagrin, could not make decisions without consulting them.

"Can you smell the sea air?" Kathryn took several fervent breaths. "It said in the brochure that it has stunning sea views from the front of the house. Apparently, this road leads us to the back."

"I'm not really fond of the sea."

"We couldn't be more different if we tried," laughed Kathryn.

"Tell me about it. I mean, look at you. You're blessed with height and slenderness and can eat *whatever* you want. Whereas I'm small and overweight! I only have to *smell* food cooking, and it goes straight onto my hips... I wonder if one of us is adopted?" she asked jokingly.

"Don't be so silly," Kathryn guffawed. "You're the double of Dad, right down to the green and amber flecks in the brown of his eyes. And you're always telling me how much like Mum I am – I have her steel grey eyes and long, dark blonde hair..." Her voice weakened into a faint whisper as she recalled the story of her birth which resulted in their mum's tragic death. "Lots of dads would have hated the child, wouldn't they?"

"Yes, they would. However, we were fortunate to have a remarkable father who loved, cared for, and protected us with all his being," she said, her voice wavering with emotion. "May he rest in peace."

"I miss him so much, but he wouldn't want us to be upset any longer than we already have."

"I know," Anna replied solemnly.

The road began to sharply turn left, and through the thinning of trees, silhouetted staggeringly against the turquoise-blue sky, where not a single cloud hung, Lyon House could now be seen displaying itself in all its finery.

Kathryn's heart started beating faster, and the hair on her body stood up at the sight before her. "It's very beautiful," she whispered.

She was so impressed that she could not speak or fully comprehend the view that presented itself in all its grandeur.

She halted the vehicle in front of an imposing, gated Gothic stone archway, which featured large black iron gate lights on either side. Leading into a walled courtyard, there was an expansive circular pond that occupied nearly the entire area, with its reflective surface extending to the enclosing low stone wall. And taking centre stage within – the house's gaze. It seemed to observe itself with an air of splendour and superiority.

Kathryn turned toward Anna and held up her hands in joyfulness. "Isn't it out of this world!" she exclaimed. "Come on; we're the first to arrive. There's no sign of Mrs Carter yet. Let's go into the courtyard and have a look round."

Anna reluctantly got out of the car and followed her sister.

They stood silently, looking up in surveyance of the mansion, whose astonishingly breathtaking architecture loomed up before them.

Raised on a terrace, towering up to five stories high and constructed of grey stone, a Neo-Gothic congregation of arches, turrets, circular conical capped towers, soaring chimney stacks, asymmetrical rooflines, and a clock tower complete with bell. To the right was a massive, elaborate conservatory. To the left, boasting its own gated entrance, a much lower set, octagonal building with matching octagonal roof.

Kathryn could scarcely breathe. She wished her father could be here to see this – a working man, he made his fortune buying run down period properties, renovating, then selling them. Some he could not bear to part with, so rented them. She had inherited her love of fine old buildings from him, and would be *so* proud of her if he were here. So proud.

Chapter 2

Kathryn and Anna sat quietly on the stone wall that framed the pond. Kathryn was still lost in her thoughts as she gazed lovingly at the house. Anna had been right – she *had* fallen instantly in love with the property.

Anna impatiently looked at her watch. "She's late. This isn't good business practice."

"I'm sure there's a reasonable explanation as to why. She'll be here soon. I'm sure of it."

"I'm bored, let's go and peek in through the windows," Anna said as she sprang up from the wall.

"No, don't. I don't want to see inside yet. I want to wait for Mrs Carter and view it properly."

"It's your house; suit yourself," Anna sighed, hopping onto the pond wall and skipping away.

"Yes," Kathryn smiled. "It *is* my house, isn't it." She clasped her hands together in elation, then turned round and gazed into the pond. "I wonder how deep it is?"

"Only a few feet probably."

"Be careful. You don't want to fall and get hurt."

"I'll be fine. Remember how great a gymnast I was at school?"

"Yes, I do," she smiled with amusement. "But that was a long time ago. You're much older now."

"Oh, stop. I'm only forty. Life *begins* at forty; doesn't it?"

"So they say... I wonder if there's any fish in it?" She leaned down, closer to the surface, searching. Not a single leaf, nor piece of debris rested upon its glossy surface. "I can't see anything. Be careful, the waters dark, which means it could be deep."

"Or just dirty and needs a good clean."

"Hmm, I suppose so. That'll have to be one of the jobs on my 'to-do list', won't it."

"Yes, it will, on perhaps page one thousand!" laughed Anna. "Kathryn, are you *sure* about this place? You're going to have a million and one things to do. Literally. It's going to be a never-ending task upkeeping this place – it's massive for just one person."

"I've never been more sure about anything in my life." She looked back toward the house, closed her eyes, then opened them gradually as if proving to herself that this was no dream.

It was real, and it was hers.

Well, it would be as soon as Mrs Carter arrived.

She tilted her head slightly to one side, listening intently. "Did you hear that?"

"Hear what?"

"I'm not sure. It's very distant, like thundering. Do you not hear it?"

"No. But I *do* see a car approaching. Hopefully, this is Mrs Carter."

Kathryn quickly stood up, excitement taking over her as it did a child on Christmas morning. "At last! I'm so excited!"

"Yes, I know. But don't let *her* see that. She'll add thousands more onto the price."

Kathryn gasped in shock. "Do you really think she would do such a thing?"

"Yes, I do. These estate agents are merciless. And they lie. You must be one step ahead of them. Pretend you aren't that keen on the house."

"I can't hide how much I like it," she said, dismayed. "She'll see it in my face how much I love it already. Plus, she was so nice on the phone."

"I bet she was," Anna scoffed.

"Well, we'll soon see. And just look at all the paperwork. I hope the contract for the house is included in all of that."

Anna laughed knowingly. "I have no doubt *at* all that it won't be."

Mrs Carter hurried toward them; concern spread over her face. "Do be careful near there, my dears. It's deeper than it looks. I dare say the bottom of it hasn't seen the light of day, nor ever will. Come to think of it; some say it's bottomless, that it's connected to an underwater river that flows under the property and out to the ocean. If you drop something in there, no doubt it'll be lost forever." She extended her hand to Kathryn. "Miss White, is it? I'm Mrs Carter; we've spoken on the telephone numerous times. I'm so sorry to be late – it's not like me at all – I forgot the keys to Lyon House, so had to go back to the office. I was halfway here too."

"It doesn't matter, you're here now, and with the most important of things – the keys," she laughed. "It's wonderful to finally meet you and be here at long last. Please, call me Kathryn. And this is Anna, my sister."

"Very pleased to meet you, dear."

"You too, Mrs Carter," Anna replied as she jumped down from the wall – much to the relief of Mrs Carter.

"Oh, dear; you did give me a fright when I saw you on that wall. I'm seventy-three you know; you gave me quite a turn."

Mrs Carter's white-blonde hair was loosely secured at the back with a neat little bun that sat comfortably at the nape of her neck.

For her age, Kathryn noticed an abundance of youth and alertness in her deep blue, almost navy eyes.

"Don't worry, Mrs Carter," Kathryn replied calmly. "I'll make sure my sister stays away from that pond."

"Thank you, dear." She began fumbling around in her handbag till the rustling and clinking of multiple sets of keys could be heard. "Here they are. Are you ready to go in?"

"Oh, yes. I've never been more ready for anything in my entire life!"

"Wonderful, dear. Truth be told, I've been looking forward to this day too. I love this house and haven't been inside for quite some time. No need you see. Not till you contacted the firm with an offer of buying the place. Straight away, I wanted to be the agent to deal with you. I may be old, dear, but my love of old houses and their histories is a passion of mine."

"Mine too," exclaimed Kathryn.

"Viewed from any angle, the house is certainly an imposing building, don't you think?"

"Very imposing," Anna chipped in sarcastically.

"Oh, look," Kathryn sang out as she noticed a series of small waves begin to form on the other side of the pond. "Ripples. I guess there *are* fish in there after all."

But for one mad, fleeting moment, she could have sworn she saw a large grey dog bent beside the pond, drinking.

The sisters walked with Mrs Carter into the stone porch entrance of the house, which had a Gothic arch and a slate roof. The entrance was eighteen feet high and extended seventeen feet into the courtyard.

Kathryn watched with eager, full, and steady eyes as Mrs Carter slowly inserted the sizeable, decorative key into the lock of the huge double wooden doors that were studded rhythmically with aged iron.

They groaned and cracked with heaviness as Mrs Carter pushed them open.

Abruptly, an aroma of aged mustiness wafted through the air and mingled with the wind that had suddenly arisen outside. It evoked memories of returning to school after the summer holidays – the scent that greeted all students – a closed-in odour: The books, the chalk, the walls, the floors, and the furniture.

It smelled antiquated and untouched, and she found it appealing. She perceived herself as privileged, being one of only three individuals inhaling the air of a house that had not been breathed in by any living being for an indeterminate period.

"Don't worry about the smell, dear. A good blast of fresh air throughout the house will clear it away in no time at all."

"Oh, I don't mind it. I find it comforting."

"From the vestibule, we enter the grand hallway," Mrs Carter cooed out proudly. "Isn't it superb."

"Oh, yes! It is! It truly is, isn't it, Anna?"

"Hmm, if you like this sort of thing."

"I *love* this sort of thing."

Directly ahead of them, taking up most of the wall, was a prominent, exquisitely carved stone Gothic arched fireplace, complete with Gothic mantlepiece.

The lower half of the walls were panelled with dark oak. And above the panelling were richly painted murals depicting scenes of angels and lions.

These images spilt over and onto the lofty ceiling covering its expanse, bringing it to life with fighting lions, and angelic, peaceful looking angels.

The doors, also dark oak, Gothic arch in shape, mirrored and framed by smooth grey stone.

On the right, a built-in three-manual organ, its pipes reaching as high as the ceiling.

Broad wooden floorboards with metal tongue and groove coated the floor.

"My God!" Kathryn finally burst out.

"It certainly claims its name, doesn't it, dear?" smiled Mrs Carter. "The wooden flooring, of course, runs throughout the house, as does the wooden wall panelling which consists of oak, cedarwood, teakwood, mahogany, and chestnut. All rooms have the same soaring ceilings and themed murals as you see here. All the fireplaces and doorways lend to the same Gothic fashion as again, you see here. And every one of the exhaustive amounts of windows are of course, mullioned."

"I'm amazed. And this is only the hall," beamed Kathryn.

"Grand. Grand hall, dear," Mrs Carter corrected.

"Of course," laughed Kathryn. "Grand hall. And this organ. How unusual it is."

"I think you'll find nothing 'usual' about this house, Miss White. You'll find a formidable home in Lyon House. If I could afford it, I would live here in a flash."

"Feel free to call on me for a cup of tea anytime you like. You'll be very welcome."

"Why, thank you, dear. That's very kind of you. I'll take you up on that."

"I'll look forward to it. We can chat away to our heart's content about this house and our passion for it, and others like it."

"Yes. We'll have much to chat away about I'm sure," she laughed.

"So," Anna pressed. "Why an organ in the grand hallway, Mrs Carter?"

"Well, why ever not, dear? Back in the Victorian times when the house was built, no expense was spared. Its owners and architects at the time were very forward-thinking, and every luxury one could ever imagine catered for. Also, back then, as is now, what a staggering topic of conversation it would've been. *And* such a wow factor, which of course is the reason behind all affluence, do you not think, dear?"

"I suppose you have a point there," Anna replied, feeling put in her place.

"When was the house built, Mrs Carter?" Kathryn asked.

"1869. By 1871 it was complete."

"Wow. They must have worked hard to build this place in such a short duration of time. Everything is so, so intricately finished."

"Oh yes, they didn't cut corners. Back then they knew what it meant to construct a fine building such as this."

"They certainly did. And I commend them all."

As they turned left to exit the grand hallway, Mrs Carter went on. "The house has its own heating and ventilation system, its own water supply, and drainage, and even boasts an extravagant electrical set-up, all of which are in the basement. I can send you a man out from the village to show you the workings of them, dear. I'm afraid things like that go over my head," she laughed. "Continuing down this corridor, we have a cloakroom and W.C, and down those stairs is the basement. I won't show it to you if you don't mind, dear; the cold you see. No good for my chest."

"Of course. I'll look forward to exploring it in my own time."

"Thank you, dear. You're such a lovely girl."

Kathryn looked across at Anna, and smiled as if to say, 'I told you she was a nice lady'.

Anna returned Kathryn's smile with nothing more than an eye-roll, then went on to quietly follow Mrs Carter and her sister.

They descended some wide, dark wood stairs, then across a corridor and into the kitchen.

"It's quite something, isn't it, dear?"

Kathryn simply stood still and silent, her eyes wide and bright as they roamed round the kitchen.

"It's octagonal in shape," Mrs Carter articulated. "With the table in the centre to match. It was constructed right here in this room by the finest of artisans. Of course, it wasn't this shade then. I'm not sure of the wood, but I am sure it would've been dark, in keeping with the rest of the house. And just look at it now, scrubbed clean so many times it's white."

"Backbreaking work no doubt," said Anna.

"Oh yes, indeed it was. But they must have loved their job. The state of the table is a conviction to that."

At last, Kathryn found her voice. "It is. It's perfect! It even has drawers." She strolled round the table, her fingers floating subtly over its smooth edges.

The kitchen, and indeed, the table, were enormous. Sixteen people could be seated comfortably around it.

Kathryn regarded the rest of the kitchen with fascination.

All the upper walls were filled with windows that reached as high as the vaulted ceiling.

She envisaged all the cook's pots and pans hanging down on sturdy chains, clanging in unison as one was removed from the rest. She could see the kitchen staff fluttering about preparing food on the many counters that fit snugly to the walls. And built into them, were ranges and cupboards.

The fireplace perfectly replicated the entryway to the kitchen, and steps led down from the kitchen via a prolific, church-like stained glass door, and into an enclosed private yard.

She breathed deeply as she imagined sitting before a prestigious fire, clutching a mug of delicious hot chocolate firmly to her chest whilst daydreaming from out of one of the many splendent windows. The light they allowed in was both bright and serene. But in her thoughts, it was dark, rainy, and miserable. Oh, how she loved to be warm and tranquil inside whilst watching the weather do its worst.

It had taken the length of her thoughts to complete the circumference of the table, whilst Mrs Carter and Anna watched on, soundlessly.

"Why is the kitchen so far away from the rest of the house, Mrs Carter?" Kathryn inquired.

"Oh, how wonderful!" Mrs Carter grasped her hands together in jubilation and smiled. "An historical question! Back in them days, dear, it was considered the height of bad manners to have kitchen smells wafting through the house. Oh, how they hated it. So, the kitchen blocks were built purposely as far away from the main house as was possible; whilst still providing easy access for the servants of course."

"I like the smell of food cooking. As you can see." Anna patted her slightly rotund stomach and laughed.

Kathryn chuckled as she made her way toward one of the windows that overlooked the rear of the house.

From where she was standing, she could just make out the meeting of the cliff-edge and sky. Stretching out towards that was the most perfectly smooth carpet of velveteen lawn she had ever encountered. It looked as though it had been pristinely sprayed on in the most perfect shade of green one could ever think a lawn to be.

"I'm not sure I like that."

Anna's eyes lit up.

At last, she sees sense!

"What is it, dear?" asked Mrs Carter, concerned.

"The sudden drop of the garden, out to nowhere."

"Oh, my dear! That's the sea!" she cried out excitedly.

"The sea?"

"Yes. The family that built the house refused to have their sea view impaired by a wall."

"The sea," Kathryn exclaimed with a hint of excitement. "Anna, the sea! I didn't realise it was so close. I love watching the sea."

"But what about the fog? It rolls in from the sea suddenly, *and* without warning, in all seasons. Not just in winter, you know."

"Oh, Anna. You don't know it, but you're talking me *further* into buying the house. Don't you remember how much I love fog?" She turned away from Anna to look at Mrs Carter. "Dull, dark, foggy, and rainy days are my thing."

"It would appear this house was made especially for you, Miss White."

"Please, do call me Kathryn," she insisted.

Chapter 3

The rest of the house seemed to go by in a dreamlike daze as Kathryn was swept through the place in a constant, spellbinding state of bliss. She was enchanted beyond words with Lyon House and already overwhelmed with love for the place. Nothing Mrs Carter could divulge to her about the house would ever make her hate, or indeed, love it more.

From the kitchen, Mrs Carter showed the girls the pantry, coal and ashes cupboards, scullery, larder, dairy, wash house and drying room.

Then leaving the kitchen wing, another W.C was situated at the end of the corridor. And as they rose the stairs, a servery, butler's pantry, and linen store could be found.

Going back towards the grand hall was a dining room with a large, recherche stained-glass window depicting a medieval, idealised view of lions feasting on the body of an angel.

The angel's face was not one of pain, horror, or mortification as one would expect, but rather one of sorrow and disappointment.

And although macabre, Kathryn fully understood its meaning and concept, which was, of course, a feast, hence its prominence within the dining room. And the lions represented strength, courage, wealth, and power. So, to feast upon an angel of *all* things was an act of considerable might.

A long, wide, highly polished dark wood table was situated centrally and ran to almost the same extent as the large room. Five generous, sumptuous dining chairs – each one boasting arms and a high-back, were placed down each length, with one taking precedence either end of the table. They were all positioned exactly one chair width apart, to avoid any unnecessary clashing of elbows with one's neighbour whilst one ate.

Next, the library – countless bookshelves rose ceiling high on all walls.

Kathryn anticipated all the great books that once were there.

She must visit some antique bookshops and fill up this library again. Bring it back to life!

As if Mrs Carter had read her mind, she stated. "In here, works of Dickens, Shakespeare, and Walter Scott filled the shelves. Many scientific and historical volumes too. And, a copy of the Koran."

From the library was the ante-room, and then came the drawing room. Its massive bay window spilt out onto the terrace, which gave way to the gardens and cliff edge.

Kathryn settled herself midpoint in the room, spread out her arms to her sides, and turned unhurriedly round and around, smiling.

She did not care what Anna and Mrs Carter thought. This room was so huge, welcoming and friendly, and had an air of peace and tranquillity to it. Up to now, this was by far her favourite room, knocking even the kitchen down to second place. The atmosphere was brimming with such a feeling of placidity; it was profuse, and it was profound.

"Back then, in the bay window, there would've been a grand piano. No doubt a stunning Gothic revival model."

"I wish I could see it as it was back then. Though you *are* painting quite the picture for my imagination."

"Come along, dear. There's so much more to see yet," Mrs Carter spoke out eagerly.

Exiting the room and turning left, colossal glass double doors separated the glass-topped orangery from the rest of the house. As the women walked, their footsteps clanked and fluctuated as they made their way across the iron grated floor that was now inflamed with rust. And etched within the wall to the left, were four large, broad, arched windows.

And then, there it was – the conservatory – eighty-one feet in length, forty foot wide and twenty-six feet high. The floor featured an intricately crafted stone mosaic, echoing the celebrated designs of Roman pavements and villa interiors. Within the space, five imposing marble statues of Greek gods stood proudly on elegant pedestals, their presence adding a grand, classical aura.

Original works of some considerable wealth thought Kathryn as she looked across to Anna, who was actually smiling as she gazed skyward through the glass roof.

"This is almost as large as the house itself," Kathryn said.

"Oh, I know, dear. Isn't it remarkable? Quite awe-inspiring really."

Kathryn took a deep breath, struggling to believe this wasn't just a selfish dream.

"In its day," Mrs Carter went on, "It was filled with araucaria, dracaenas, and aurelias. Victorians thought those the height of fashion you know. They would also have had African Fern, and lapageria that would climb to the roof! All the plants were well chosen to fill out the conservatory. It would look silly with little plants dotted about; don't you think?"

"Of course." Kathryn nodded in agreement as she replied.

"Planted for the delectation of the eyes, there would've been eucalyptus, camellias, yuccas, and numerous other collections of ornamental plants. The passageway we entered the conservatory by is known as the orangery, due to its being lined with orange trees."

"I'm overjoyed you know so much about the place!"

"As I said, it's a passion of mine. Going back toward the orangery is the potting shed. Do you like to garden, dear?"

"No, not really. I'm more of an indoor sort of person. But on the occasion I *do* venture out, I like nothing more than to appreciate a fine, immaculately kept garden."

"Oh, Miss White. Sorry, Kathryn dear. In its prime, this house's gardens were kept to an impeccably high standard.

Covering its three hundred acres were a wealth of lawns and woodlands, gardens, flowers, rose beds and shrubbery. There were stables, orchards, vineries, and fruit trees. Kitchen walled gardens and greenhouses that grew every fruit and vegetable one could ever comprehend. There were hot and cold orchard houses, a rose house, gardeners' bothies, and numerous fishponds, and even had a boating lake and boathouse. There were farms on the land too, *and* lodges. But of course, all that's gone now," Mrs Carter concluded sadly.

"What happened?" Kathryn asked.

"A firm by the name of 'Holton and East' bought the estate in the 1970s with the intention of building holiday homes for the wealthy, with it being so close to the ocean you see, dear. The farms, lodges, and all outbuildings were demolished, the boating lake drained and levelled off. Everything; everything gone." She had a faraway look as she clutched at the pearls round her neck.

With a quizzical look, Anna asked, "so, what happened? Why didn't the plans for the holiday homes go ahead?"

Mrs Carter cleared her throat before responding. "My dear, I think that should be a story for another day, do you not think? We still have many more things to see, and just look at the time."

"I hope we aren't keeping you from another appointment?" Kathryn asked, concerned.

"Not at all, Miss, I'm sorry – Kathryn. I'm simply set in my ways. I have tea at three, you see," she ended with a laugh.

"Well, perhaps when we've finished the viewing, I could treat you to afternoon tea in the village? I'd love to hear more about the house. After all, I'll become the next chapter of its book sorta speak, won't I?" she replied, excitedly.

"You will indeed, dear. Thank you. I know a quaint little place in the village. Quiet too, so we shan't be disturbed."

"It sounds delightful," she beamed. "Doesn't it, Anna?"

"Hmm? Oh, yes," she replied, disinterested. And with a splash of sarcasm upon her face, "delightful."

"And now we return down the orangery and corridor, and into the staircase hall. The grand staircase is 'L' shaped, complete with a meticulously carved opulent wooden bannister."

Two striking, church-like stained glass windows framed the staircase eloquently. Kaleidoscopic stains of light danced elegantly and lustrously over the wooden stairs, then down to a leap of speckles upon the floor. It all purposely caught the eye, leading you to the huge mural on the wall that stood before the foot of the staircase. It depicted a man on a white charger that reared up on its hind legs.

Kathryn's heart seemed to stand still, the entire world with it.

Mrs Carter's voice faded away into nothingness, till only she and the mural before her remained. If the world had dropped suddenly from beneath her feet, she would not have noticed, she would not have cared.

This man facing her, this beautiful man that seemed to stare intently back at her, had the most vivid, bluest eyes she had ever seen, or could conceive.

Was it the dancing opulence of colours from the stained glass that rent his eyes so blue?

Within them, there was a universe of undiscovered hues so bright and stunning that she could not breathe. They penetrated her very soul.

"He's very handsome, isn't he, dear?"

Unbeknownst to Mrs Carter, she had punctured the ethereal world that Kathryn and the mural had slipped.

Responding as if emerging from deep slumber, Kathryn replied with evident fatigue. "Hmm?"

"Roman Lyons. He was most handsome. Don't you think, dear?"

"Yes, Mrs March," she answered in a slow, languorous tone. "Breathtakingly so."

"Carter, Mrs Carter, dear," she sternly corrected before setting off away from the girls and down another corridor, talking as she went.

"Who's Mrs March?" Anna whispered to Kathryn with an enquiring face.

"I've no idea. I hope she wasn't offended," she said worryingly. "I didn't even realise I was saying it."

"Well, I'm sure she's forgotten about it already, just listen to her, she's in her element here. She's talking away and doesn't even realise we aren't following her," she chuckled. "And as for him," she said as she looked up at the portrait. "I'm afraid you're over a hundred years too late for this man. This, Roman Lyons."

Kathryn sighed heavyheartedly as she allowed Anna to take her by the arm and lead her down the corridor after the still talking Mrs Carter.

"... And this is the office. Isn't that church style window exquisite, my dears? Opposite we have the billiard room, complete with the original billiard table. I'm not sure what became of the balls though, dear, *or* cues. Cues, is that what they're called? Or is it sticks? I can never remember."

"I think either or can be used," Anna said with a smile.

"Thank you, dear. And lastly for downstairs, we have the workshop, which then leads off to a W.C..." Her voice trailed away as she inspected Kathryn, who had not uttered a single word since viewing the mural. "My dear, are you all right? You look dreadfully flushed."

"She's quite well. She's just overcome with passion. In more ways than one," Anna said with a giggle.

Kathryn shot Anna a look of feigned amazement, before saying, "my sister's right. I can honestly and doubtlessly admit just how passionate I feel about this house and how in love with it I am. If, of course, it *is* possible to fall in love with bricks and mortar."

Mrs Carter rushed over to Kathryn. "My dear; of course it is. I believe houses have a soul; you know."

"Me too," Kathryn agreed ecstatically. "I fell in love with this place at first sight. Though Anna said I should keep it to myself."

"There's no shame in it, Anna dear. No shame at all."

Anna raised her eyebrows at Kathryn, who was smiling mischievously back at her.

Why, I do believe Kathryn's just 'turned the tables' on me. I'm going to have to watch these two with their overly romanticised view of this house. It all seems far too good to be true. *Far* too good.

Chapter 4

Once upstairs and off the landing, Mrs Carter stood looking first to the left, and then to the right. The long, wide corridor stretched out before them, leaving the explorer uncertain of their direction.

"I think we'll go this way first, dears."

Turning to the right and directly ahead of them, there was a beguiling floor to ceiling church-style Gothic stained-glass window. It's flurry of colours pranced down and seeped into the wooden floors below, to then diffuse splendiferously away.

They entered what was to be Kathryn's bedroom through the boudoir, which contained a discreet toilet. And much to Kathryn's delight, a large bay window that looked out over the conservatory. It held within its frame stunning views of hills and trees that gracefully danced within the breeze.

Situated to the right in the corner of the room was a grand fireplace.

Through a doorway – the bedroom, with two large windows that overlooked the lawns, cliff edge, and ocean. To the left of the room, another prominent fireplace was situated in the corner.

"This is all so beautiful, isn't it, Anna? I can't wait to fall asleep by firelight."

"You can do that quite easily back at home."

"Yes, I know. But this is in the bedroom. A bedroom! It's all so perfect!"

"Through here is the master bedroom's bathroom," Mrs Carter said. "It too has a fireplace."

"In the bathroom?!" Kathryn almost shrieked out in glee.

"Oh, yes, dear. All the rooms have fireplaces. There's even one in the linen store at the other end of the house."

"Oh, my God," Kathryn said as she flitted past the genial Mrs Carter.

Kathryn seated herself on the edge of the bath. She was overawed. She did not think that she could feel any more euphoric than what she was feeling now. But the house, so it would seem, was a *constant* state of rapture. As each room, and so too, nook and cranny revealed itself to her, the level of intoxication she felt seemed to grow with each breath she took.

She wished the viewing were over.

She wished she had already moved in.

She wished that she could just... Be. She was seduced beyond sense.

"All baths, basins, and toilets were brought into being from the finest of porcelain, my dear," Mrs Carter began again. And in doing so, brought Kathryn from out of her thoughts.

"Is there anyone else interested in the house?"

"No, dear. Just you."

"But why?" she asked, bewildered. "This place is astonishing. It's structurally sound, well-kept. And, cheap."

With a furrowed brow and shaking of her head, Anna shot Kathryn a look of 'shut up'.

She did not want Kathryn to leave home and would miss her desperately. But she also wanted her to be happy, and it would make her happy if Kathryn could buy this house, *and* for the price it was worth. Not a *penny* more.

"People just don't have the money nowadays for the upkeep of such a big house like this one, dear."

"True," smiled Kathryn. "The people that keep the land will stay on, won't they?"

"Why, of course, dear, yes. If that's what you'd like. I'm sure they'll be relieved to know they won't lose their jobs."

"Oh, Heavens, no! Of course not. Like I said before, I adore the beauty of gardens and all they have to bring. But, when it comes to *getting* them that way, well," she laughed. "That isn't my cup of tea."

Mrs Carter licked her lips at the mention of the word tea. "Oh, Kathryn, our tea! We must hurry along, my dears. I'm expected at three. My routine, you know." She hurriedly looked at her watch. "Two-fifteen. We've just enough time to see the rest of the house."

Once back onto the corridor, Mrs Carter accelerated through another bedroom complete with dressing room, and W.C. Then a further two bedrooms, and linen store. And bringing the almost infinite corridor to a close, there were two more bedrooms.

Retreating up the corridor, to the right was a bathroom, box and storeroom, dressing room, two more bedrooms. Then back to where they had commenced – the landing and staircase, with the ninth and final bedroom completing the cycle.

"All nine bedrooms are pleasantly spacious, aren't they, dear?"

"They are," Kathryn agreed, smiling.

"Oh, my dear, I completely forgot," she said, as she dashed off back down along the corridor. "This staircase," she persisted, ardently, "leads up to the second floor. This is the first, downstairs the ground, and then the basement of course." She beckoned Kathryn and Anna to follow her up the narrower, but still phenomenally made staircase. "Up here, we have many bedrooms and bathrooms. For the servants, dear. Though now we would address them as staff, wouldn't we?"

"We would," Kathryn agreed.

"Will you have any staff, my dear?" Mrs Carter asked as she followed Kathryn into one of the bedrooms.

"No," she turned to face Mrs Carter. "Just the people to look after the land please. I'll take on some cleaners once a week to help me keep on top of things."

"Oh, how splendid! You'll be placing an ad in the local shop, I take it? I love creating jobs for our own!"

"Yes, of course. It'll be the first thing I do the moment I move in."

"You'll be living here alone then, will you, dear?"

"I will. Oh, Anna, look. The view of the ocean is wonderful from up here. Come see." She turned and gestured Anna towards her.

The sea was scintillating. The sun shone its blazing light into it, creating auroral silver cusps on the tips of the waves that bounced and bobbed peacefully within.

"Isn't it beautiful," Kathryn sighed out contentedly.

Chapter 5

When the viewing was complete and the doors to Lyon House once again closed and securely locked, Mrs Carter gave fluid instructions and directions of the whereabouts of the Café in which they were to meet. It was in the park, she had said. 'Myrtle Park Café' was its name, and renowned all around for its pretty little Vintage-Esque afternoon teas – of which she was a proud patron. Their best customer, she had beamed.

After one last, longing look at the house, Kathryn finally climbed into the car and sighed dreamily. "Oh, have you ever seen such beauty. And the artistry. All the creative, hardworking people that put their time and energy into completing this remarkable building. I wish I could've seen it how it was back then – all furnished grandiosely and deluxe."

"You should do your best to recreate it. I'm sure you could pick up all sorts of things from reclamation yards. Online even. I'll look too, see what I can find."

"Oh, would you?! Thank you. I know you don't want me to live here, so that means a lot to me."

"I want you to be happy. So would Dad."

Tears sprang to both their eyes.

"He would. And, Anna, he would *love* this house. I know that I have his blessing in buying it."

"You do. In fact, if he were alive, he'd be moving in with you, I'm sure of it," she said to bring a smile to Kathryn's lips.

"Yes. And you'd have to come too," she laughed.

"Kicking and screaming."

"You don't like anything that predates your birth, do you?" she giggled.

"No. You're right. I don't suppose I do. Come on, we must be off. Mrs Carter left at least ten minutes ago. You wouldn't want her to sell the house to anyone else now, would you?"

"God, no," Kathryn replied, firmly.

"Come on then, tea and history await us, much to my disdain," she said, pulling a torturous look across her face. "But then, seeing as it's afternoon tea, I can at least eat whilst you two dream about the past."

"Deal," laughed Kathryn.

As Kathryn started the car, a loud thud from the rear made them both turn, startled.

"What on earth was that?" Anna asked, her heart racing.

"I don't know. I can't see anything," Kathryn said as she looked for anything untoward in the mirrors of the car. Then she opened the door and got out.

At the back of the vehicle there lay a bright yellow ball, about the size of a tennis ball.

She picked it up and held it tightly in her hand, looking for the children she assumed had been playing with it. Or a dog walker.

But there was no one to be seen.

But, she thought, it *was* quite windy now, and the ball light. So, perhaps it had been carried some way by the wind. She would take it with her, just in case they happened upon an eager dog with an owner in tow. When she moved in, she must insist on the gates of the lion clad posts be closed and locked with a sign denoting 'Private Property' impressed upon them. She did not want any strangers to wander around. It was, or would be, soon hers, and hers alone.

She climbed back into the car and tossed the ball to Anna, who caught it with misgivings.

"Where was this?"

"It was on the ground by the back of the car."

"It wasn't there before."

"I know. But it's only light." She leaned toward Anna and tapped the ball gently. "Plastic, I think. The wind must have blown it into the car."

"But it wasn't anywhere to be seen when we were talking with Mrs Carter."

"Well, the winds picked up since then. I'm sure they'll be a poor little dog somewhere near searching for his lost ball. There you go, you see. A dog."

"What?"

"A dog. Can't you hear it? It's a dog barking. Excitedly by the sounds of it."

"I can't hear a thing."

"Wind your window down. It's getting loud now," she said as she got out of the car once again to give the poor dog its ball back.

But still, there was no one there. No dog. No owner clinging to a lead. Nothing. Only the trees whispers, swayed by the relentless whips of the wind.

"How odd," Kathryn said quietly.

"What is it?"

"There's no one around."

Anna looked at the ball that she was now rigidly clutching in her hands. She had a bad feeling about this. But for Kathryn's sake, she would keep her opinions to herself. It was, after all, just a ball.

She threw it from the window and watched as it bounced gaily away from the car.

"No dog?" Anna asked, hopefully.

"No, no dog. But then again, the wind carries sound as well as things, doesn't it?"

Anna mused for a while before answering. "Yes. I must agree with you there."

She consoled her thoughts by finding rationality in the sudden emergence of the bright little ball. Although their home was miles away from the famous Knebworth concerts, when the wind blew in a particular direction, the music, and every single word the singer's sung, could be heard as clearly as if the concert were in their very own back garden. So, yes. She would accept this possibility.

"Kathryn, it's just gone three. Mrs Carter will be waiting. And I'm hungry."

Kathryn hurriedly climbed back into the car and clicked on her seatbelt as she closed the door. "Where's the ball?"

"I've thrown it back outside. You know, in case the dog comes for it."

Kathryn nodded her head in agreement as she set off down the road and away from the house.

Had she glanced into her rearview mirror, she would have seen the ball tremble, rise as though gripped by unseen hands, and drift upward into the howling void – only to dissolve into nothingness, as if it had never existed at all.

Chapter 6

Mrs Carter was waiting anxiously outside the Myrtle Park Café for the arrival of Kathryn and Anna. When she saw them approaching, the anxiety on her old, but very well-groomed face was replaced with one of elation. "Oh, my dears! Here you are at last! Did you get lost? I was beginning to worry. Come along now; I've had my usual table all prepared and is ready for us."

She ushered the girls into the Café where smells of freshly baking cakes and bread hung delightfully in the air. Fresh coffees and worldly teas pervaded the atmosphere, making sure that all who entered were given an incredible palate for the nose and senses.

Nestled snugly within the farthest corner of the Café was an elaborate white wrought iron table with four matching chairs, on which one, lay Mrs Carter's paperwork.

Upon the table's fine glass top were plates containing pyramids of skillfully cut crust-less sandwiches and cakes. A set of matching crockery infused with a tasteful bold floral design in rich deep reds, greens, and yellows, waited patiently to be filled with all the tables' indulgences.

When all three women were seated, a large teapot, jug of milk, and a small bowl containing crisp white sugar cubes were quickly set down before them.

"Oh, Mrs Carter, this is lovely!" Kathryn said as she plopped two sugar cubes into her milky tea. "Thanks so much for letting us join you. I can see why you come here daily," she enthused.

"Oh, yes. All the girls here know my little ways you know," she laughed. "They know something would be dreadfully amiss if I were not here at three," she finished with a smile and sip of her tea. "Do help yourself to a sandwich, dear," she said to Anna. "Meat pate and finely cut cucumber I believe them to be today. And the cakes! Oh, how scrumptious. Fresh cream too! My favourite," she exclaimed as she cautiously removed a fresh cream and jam scone from the meticulously constructed pyramid. And in doing so, making the precariously set out structure, falter.

Anna had overfilled her plate with sandwiches and a selection of butterfly buns.

Kathryn was far too exhilarated to eat, preferring instead to watch the going's on of nature outside, therefore allowing Anna and Mrs Carter to be enraptured by the almost picture-perfect abundance of delights.

Torn and shredded clouds seared their way through the blue sky as the wind blew gently. The leaves of a nearby tree shivered in the slight breeze, revealing silvery veined undersides.

She watched as the first leaf loosened and broke free, heralding the beginning of autumn. It slowly shimmied and spiralled down to rest upon a bush below.

"Are you not eating, Kathryn dear?" Mrs Carter asked.

"Oh, no; thank you. I'm not very hungry. Too excited about the house you see."

"Oh, my dear," Mrs Carter smiled, "that's perfectly understandable. Shall we get to it then? Our little historical chat about the house?" She clinked her cup back down into its saucer and began rummaging through her paperwork. "But first, here is the contract of sale, my dear. Would you like to check it over?"

"Oh, no. That won't be necessary."

"Kathryn," Anna broke in, concerned.

"Anna, it's perfectly all right. Besides, my solicitor's already gone over a copy of the contract that Mrs Carter kindly emailed over prior to us coming here today."

"You never mentioned it."

"No, I didn't think it important to you at the time."

"Well, it's important to me now. May I look it over, Mrs Carter?"

"Of course you can, dear."

Mrs Carter duly handed over the contract to Anna, who set about reading every single word and tiny structured paragraph.

She had taken over the running of their father's property rental business so knew precisely what was what, and did not want Kathryn to be taken advantage of.

"Mrs Carter, while Anna's engrossed with the contract, please do begin telling me the history of the house. I'm fascinated with it all, as I'm sure you must know by now."

"Of course, my dear. But first, one more bite of this delicious scone."

And then, it came into quiddity – the whole tale of Lyon House was unfolded theatrically before Kathryn.

"As soon as the Lyon family moved into the newly built house, strange things began to occur. It was as though the house didn't want anyone to occupy it.

The then young Roman's grandfather came to visit, and sometime after the dinner bell had sounded, and the family gathered for dinner, there was no sign of the grandfather. So, of course, a servant was sent to look for him, and when the servant returned, dour news poured from their lips – he was dead. The servant had discovered his body slumped over the billiard table. A sudden heart attack the doctor had said.

Then, only a few weeks later, Roman's two younger sisters died. One of pneumonia, the other drowned in a tragic accident on the boating lake.

Shortly after, Roman's uncle – his father's brother, was severely injured when he fell from his horse while riding in the grounds. He fell in love with the nurse who tended to him, and they married the instant he was discharged from the hospital. After a few short months of bliss, he contracted and died of tuberculosis. His wife was naturally devastated of course and never got over his death, pregnant too.

When she came to her due date, both she and the child died in childbirth. Nothing could be done for either of them, too much blood loss you see. The child was asphyxiated in the womb, due to lack of oxygen with the poor woman being dead. They had to cut the unfortunate thing from out of her, but was too late."

"Oh my God! That's terrible," Kathryn said, aghast.

"Indeed. And when her brother came to Lyon House to attend the funeral, he became quite taken with one of the young servant girls, rather beautiful she was – by all accounts anyway. They very quickly became lovers, even though he had a poor unsuspecting wife at home tending to their sick child.

Needless to say, his wife became aware of the situation almost immediately. She was a countess you see, and there was nothing and no one that she didn't know. So, she left the child in the care of her faithful nanny, and, blinded by rage, set off to Lyon House.

She encountered the lovers the moment she arrived. She burst into the bedroom of the servant girl and caught them during a fit of passion, pulled out a gun and shot them both dead. She then turned the gun onto herself but miraculously survived.

After many months in the hospital she was discharged, but, to an insane asylum. You see, although her body recovered, her mind never did.

It was quite the national scandal. It was a terrible time for the Lyons to have such a scandalous interest in them. They were a very private family you see, dear.

Anyway, a few weeks later, after her admittance to the asylum, she escaped and was found wandering around the Lyon House Estate 'looking' for her husband in nothing more than a long, white hospital gown. It was raining that night too, so consequently, her long dark hair was stained black by the rain and matted to her body, and the gown almost looked like a translucent second skin. She was deathly pale, and of course, had a calm and wild look about her if you know what I mean, dear.

One of the kitchen servants was taking out some leftover foodstuffs for the pigs, when she saw this 'phantom' of a woman. The poor servant fainted in fear, but alas, upon falling to the ground, struck her head on a stone step. The wretched mite died instantaneously. She was only a young little thing too.

Well, the countess believed this poor dead girl to be her child, the one she had left in the nanny's charge, so laid beside her and nursed her in her arms whilst softly singing.

From within the house, the elderly butler, going about his duties, could hear this haunting song, so he went about himself to investigate.

On seeing this spectral woman with long, sleek black hair, cradling the body of the young blood-soaked servant, the shock of the encounter caused him to develop a sudden case of the hiccups.

He managed to get himself back into the house and alert the family of what he had discovered. But, by the time the police and doctor arrived, the countess was dead, with the young servant still clutched tightly into her. The doctor said it was pneumonia, due to her being outside in the cold wintery weather, dressed in such a manner. And as for the poor butler, his hiccups triumphed on uninterrupted until he finally hiccupped himself to death!

Fancy, dying of hiccups! Officially, the doctor said it was irritation of the gall bladder and diaphragm.

By this time, all the goings-on and deaths were becoming somewhat of a phenomenon in the county.

Word spread about all the misgivings and ghostly happenings of the house.

Soon after, the legend of Lyon House was born, or rather, as the locals and anyone who knows of its history, call it, 'The Curse of Lyon House'.

All subsequent visits to the family from friends, acquaintances, and relatives resulted in them dying suddenly in strange and mysterious circumstances.

For instance, a distant cousin came to Lyon House for a short visit while passing through on his trip further up the coast. He was enjoying a lovely game of croquet with the Master of the house whilst all the ladies watched on attentively, when suddenly, and no one witnessed precisely what had happened, so no one could *say* exactly what had occurred. But the doctor's verdict was that he died from septicemia, caused by a blow to the foot from a mallet. His poor wife was naturally distraught. And being too upset to travel home, stayed on at Lyon House to convalesce.

Soon after her husband's funeral, which took place at Lyon House, she suffered a stroke and died.

The final straw – at least for the servants – came when, in an attempt to lift the suffocating gloom that had settled over the house since its first inhabitants arrived, the men swam in the lake while the women picnicked beneath the trees.

But when all bathers had returned and were dried and dressed, there was one perduring pile of neatly folded clothes that lay unclaimed. Searches were carried out, but no one could be found. So, the poor unfortunate man was presumed drowned.

But the most bizarre thing of all, dear, all the men were accounted for. So, to whom did the clothes belong?

After that, all but the head gardener, housekeeper, and one maid stayed on. All the other servants fled in fear for their lives, and indeed, their families and friends. For it would seem all who were touched by Lyon House, were touched by death itself."

"That's quite a story," Kathryn exuded.

"Isn't it just," Mrs Carter beamed back. "It doesn't end there though, dear."

"There's more?"

"Oh, yes, dear. Much more! Eventually, young Master Roman was sent away abroad to attain the best education money could bring. In line with his parents' wishes, he was encouraged to travel the world and experience various aspects of life.

Some thirty years later, with the house seemingly settled – save for the legend that still lingered – the Master and his wife arranged to visit their son, Roman, in New York, where he'd been studying music. He'd become something of a violin virtuoso, drawing admirers from around the world eager to hear him play. It would be the first time his parents had listened to his music – and the first time they'd seen him since he left Lyon House.

But alas, it wasn't meant to be, for the ship sank on its maiden voyage, taking almost everyone with it. The Lyons were amongst those who lost their lives in that freezing, deathly cold ocean. The ones that didn't drown, froze to death in minutes! All those poor souls, dying like that. I could cry and never stop."

"Mrs Carter?" Kathryn inquired.

"Yes, dear?"

"What year was it when the ship sank?"

Mrs Carter pulled a handkerchief out of her handbag and proceeded to dab her eyes dry.

"I believe it to have been the year of 1912, dear. In April."

"It was the Titanic, wasn't it?!" Kathryn almost screeched out in amazement.

"Why, yes, dear; yes. I do believe it was."

"Of course it was!" Anna dryly boomed out as she looked up from the contract that she had tried so terribly hard to concentrate.

During Mrs Carter's remarks, she observed Kathryn closely while holding the contract, which appeared inconsequential.

Her sister had sat there, still and wide-eyed, holding on to every word of Mrs Carter's.

Was Mrs Carter trying to talk herself out of a sale? The house was beautiful; yes, of that she had to admit. It even had a pleasant atmosphere. But one could not argue the 'facts' that Mrs Carter was freely, and ecstatically, bringing to light.

There was a definite pattern going on here, and she did not like it. She was perplexed at the enormity of how much Kathryn was enamoured with the house.

The first feeling of dread had mounted within her when that ball had thudded suddenly into the back of the car. But she had, against her better judgment, allowed Kathryn to explain it all away.

But now, as she sat listening to Mrs Carter go wildly on about the doomed, macabre, and strange untimely endings of all who have lived, and all who are linked to Lyon House, she could sit silently no longer. Enough was enough. She would not allow Kathryn to buy this death house!

"I've heard enough. Kathryn, we should go," she stood abruptly from her chair. "It's getting late."

Both Kathryn and Mrs Carter looked taken aback as they turned to glance at Anna, whose skin had taken on an unsettling pallor.

"But," Kathryn protested. "I'm not finished speaking with Mrs Carter about the house yet."

"It doesn't matter. I won't let you buy it. I've a bad feeling about it. A *very* bad feeling."

"You fret too much," Kathryn said with a smile.

"And you, not enough."

"I think it's riveting."

"I'm going to consult my cards."

"You'll do no such thing," Kathryn admonished.

"But, Kathryn. From what I've heard today, what we *both* have heard, this house... it *kills* people."

"Houses don't kill people," laughed Kathryn. "Only people kill people. *Or* of course, circumstances of God, and nature."

"Or the circumstances of curses!"

"Stop the dramatics and sit down. Everything Mrs Carter has said today is just life – death comes for us all. *We* could claim we're cursed, orphaned as we are, and that I bear the blame for our mother's fate. After all, I am the child who ended her life. So perhaps... *we* really are cursed."

"Well, that's just ridiculous," Anna conceded as she re-seated herself onto the chair.

"My point exactly. 'Life' happens to us all. It's just that some of us are more afflicted than others. Does that make them all cursed? 'Life' occurs in *all* houses, ours included. Look up the history of every single home and building ever built. I'm sure you'd find plenty of 'curses' as you call them."

"Yes, I'm sure you're right. But none so grim as this."

"Pour yourself another cup of tea and relax." She patted Anna's arm lovingly. "No doubt all these tales of woe, tantalising as they are, have numerous added embellishments, care of gossipmongers. Times that by a hundred years and you end up with something rather fantastical."

She turned her attention back to Mrs Carter and resumed their conversation. "And what about Roman? What became of him? Do you know?"

"He returned home some five months later. To run the estate of course, with him being the sole heir. And, like you, dear, was very down to earth, not believing in curses, or so it was documented anyway. He too found it all an animated tale to tell over dinner."

"You see," Kathryn said to Anna. Then, addressing Mrs Carter. "Please, do go on, I'm riveted. I'm on the edge of my seat here."

"This is where it all starts to get a bit sad, dear."

"Oh, no," Kathryn said unhappily. "Why?"

"Well, he became a recluse, he never left the house again. The last remaining housemaid fled, claiming that the Master roamed the halls and corridors, raving like a madman about spectral visions only he could see. But then again, no one truly knows what happened, do they, dear? Only he holds the truth of his own fate."

"I agree wholeheartedly with you there." She cast a knowing look at Anna, who sat quietly sipping her tea, still the colour of slate. "So," Kathryn pressed. "Did Roman get a happily ever after?" She bit her bottom lip. "Did he marry?" She felt joyous at the prospect he had not, and jealous at the thought he had.

Anna shot Kathryn an 'are you kidding me' look, which made Kathryn blush.

"Do you know, my dear. That, I don't know. All I can say is, he was the last Master of Lyon House. No one knows its history from 1912 onwards. Only that the company from which you will buy the house now have owned it since the 1970s."

"Oh, yes," Anna remarked. "You never did get around to telling us the reason the holiday homes weren't built."

"Oh, my dear, yes! Well remembered!" Mrs Carter sang out. "After the land was cleared of all other buildings etc. A team of specialised masons were brought in to deal with the house, with it being such a size you see. It took them two days to drill out the foundations of the house for them to lay their explosive charges.

When all was ready, they huddled together behind the Gothic archway into the courtyard and plunged the detonator. After the blast, when all the dust had settled, they were dumbfounded to see the house still standing! And, to all appearances, completely unaffected by the explosion.

On closer inspection, there was not *one* single hair-line crack to be found anywhere! A true testament to the builders, don't you think, dear?"

"Which backs up the fact that this house isn't right!" Anna almost screamed out.

"Which backs up the fact that this house is faultlessly built," Kathryn replied, sternly. "I raise my hat to all involved in building her."

"So, this death house is a 'she' now, is it?"

"Yes." Kathryn smiled contentedly. "I do believe it is."

"Kathryn, please; I beg of you. Don't buy this house."

"Anna, please, control yourself," she ordered. "Mrs Carter, this house is indeed a testament to the builders – and to me. If I had even the slightest doubt about buying it," she glanced at Anna, "which I don't - there would be no reason, in this world or any other, to hesitate. I fell in love with it the very moment I saw it, and I will remain in love with it until the day I die."

"Oh, Kathryn, please don't say that."

"I'm sorry, but I don't believe in all that nonsense you do. Ghosts, ghouls, and things that go bump in the night are merely hysteria brought on by the hysterics of people such as yourself.

It all came about in the Victorian times you know. Your tarot cards were actually a parlor game made for entertaining the ladies after dinner while the gentlemen spoke of politics, *and* no doubt their silly ladies in the parlor room allowing a game to shape and dictate their decisions in life. *I*, am *not* one of those ladies."

So, that was it. Kathryn had made up her mind.

Anna sat there and watched in bewilderment as her sister signed all the necessary paperwork to become the proud, but next ill-fated owner of Lyon House.

She had signed her life away, and with that, her fate was sealed.

She had tried to stop her, but it seemed that the more she spoke out against the house, the more intent Kathryn had become in buying it. All she could do was hope Kathryn was right, that she was indeed a 'silly believer of nonsense'.

Anna excused herself, saying she needed to pay a visit to the ladies' room. And while there she unzipped her handbag, reached inside, and pulled out a pack of carefully wrapped tarot cards. She deftly removed the white satin cloth and placed it onto the closed toilet lid.

She shuffled the cards slowly, all the while whispering to herself, "prove me wrong... Prove me wrong. Please. Prove me wrong."

Each time she drew a card from countless amounts of shuffles; the same card would always be uncloaked.

It answered her query simply, and concisely...

Death...

Death...

Death.

Chapter 7

October 1st heralded Kathryn's arrival to Lyon House. Several large removal trucks had unloaded their contents, and the house filled with an eclectic collection of eloquent vintage and period-style furnishings sympathetic to the house.

Mrs Carter had telephoned Kathryn to say that a man from the village would be arriving the following day to show her how to operate the heating system, along with various other contraptions needed to obtain the smooth running of the house.

By the evening's end, Kathryn lay on the bed exhausted, the darkened room brought to life only by the fire that burned tremendously within the confines of its place.

She was finally here.

A smile spread about her face as she watched the angels and lions above her, strangely animated by the blaze of the spitting, cracking fire.

She felt she would not need extra heating for the house. Its thick walls were perfect insulation that held into its breast every atom of heat from the sunlight's rays that beamed through the windows. The boisterous blazing fire had been lit purely for ambience.

She lay for hours, entertained and lost in the simplicity of the wandering shadows as they unfolded and danced upon the walls.

Then slowly, she drifted off to sleep.

It was three o'clock in the morning when she awoke.

The darkness pressed in – deep, suffocating, almost absolute. Then came the silence, so profound that the only sound she could hear was a thin, high-pitched hiss lingering in the air, like something unseen watching, waiting.

She got out of bed and slowly made her way towards the window, opened it, and breathed in the fragrance of the night air.

She sat on the window seat and gazed out to sea.

How menacing it looked on this moonless, starless night; so black, so vast, so... foreboding. Unearthly even. If at any point in time, it determined to rise and engulf the world, God himself could not stop it.

The ocean and sky faded seamlessly together so perfectly that one could not discern one from the other, giving the illusion of being entombed by the sea, or indeed, imprisoned by the sky. It had become one complete entity, its vastness never-ending, one absolute, endless black void.

She stayed seated for a good while, enjoying the aura of the house and its surroundings at night. It was so startlingly peaceful.

The one thing that endured – breaking through the strange, muted barrier – was the lullaby of the sea. 'Shhhhh... Shhhhh... Shhhhh,' it whispered, slow and serene. Hypnotic. Transcendent. A splendorous melody that cradled her as she drifted back to bed.

As she gravitated towards sleep, she wondered if it would be the darkness of the sea or the blackness of the night that would embody her dreams.

By the time sleep's heavy embrace claimed her, she remained oblivious to the apparition – a man hovering mere inches from her face, his hollow gaze fixed upon her as she slumbered, undisturbed.

Chapter 8

The following morning a dense fog sat upon the house, and Kathryn was awoken by the droll, melancholy sound of communicating ships far out at sea. She had left the window open last night, which had given way to a slight, misty bearing about the room. She slept deeply – one of the best nights of rest she'd had in quite some time, not since her father's passing. She wondered how well Anna had slept. Their goodbye had been tearful, and last night marked the first time they each faced life alone. But she relished solitude, never needing companionship to ward off boredom – unlike poor Anna.

She was fearful of Anna having regular gatherings and surrounding herself with 'like-minded' people. Her obsession with tarot cards, Mediums and Psychics was becoming unhealthy. She had functioned as Anna's anchor whilst at home. But now she did not know what would become of her sister. And she was sure that Anna felt the same thing about her.

∞ ∞ ∞

The small but strong-looking man from the village arrived at eleven o'clock on the dot. He introduced himself as Mr Woodsman, and informed Kathryn that he was to be the new gardener. Mr Day, the previous gardener, had been taken ill, so had chosen to begin his retirement early.

She expressed her get well wishes and asked him to compliment Mr Day on all the excellent work he had done – the grounds had been kept to a level of untarnished pristine.

"It's a fine house you have here, Miss White."

"Isn't it beautiful? I find myself smiling all the time – how lucky I am to be its patron. Please, come in, and bring your dog as well. This cold and fog are hardly good for any living creature's lungs, wouldn't you say?" she laughed.

"Dog?" he asked, a confused look in his burnt oak eyes.

"Yes, I heard its barks a while ago."

"I have no dog, Miss White."

"Oh, I'm so sorry, I assumed it to be yours. I must have a stray in the grounds." She closed the door behind him with a shiver. "I'll show you the way to the basement. Though I haven't ventured down there yet, so it'll be a surprise to us both," she laughed.

He followed her through the grand hall, down the corridor, then down the stairs to the basement.

"Oh, look," she exclaimed. "It's not as dark and damp as Mrs Carter led me to believe. Just look at this."

Within the bowels of the basement, which stretched to the entire range of the house, vaulted brick ceilings accommodated a servants' hall, and a labyrinth of all the expected offices.

"You could get lost down here," he said.

"You could. Mrs Carter didn't give you a map by any chance, did she?" she laughed.

"No, but she *did* tell me everything I needed would be in the first room I came to. Apparently 'for the convenience of the household.'"

"And ours, so it would seem."

"Here we are look," he said, after opening the first door.

Inside the room was an industrial-sized, complex-looking machine.

Kathryn had at once concluded to leave Mr Woodsman to his tinkering. Her being there would only hinder any progress he made.

She must remember to take his telephone number. He seemed as though he were a jack of all trades, and her being alone out here, she would never know when a situation would arise in which his services would be required.

"Would you like a cup of tea?"

"Oh, yes! That would be lovely. Thank you. Milky please, two sugars."

"Coming right up."

Fifteen minutes later, his tea was delivered.

He accepted it thankfully and began regaling to her the problems he was having in getting the heating system going – it had ceased up through lack of use. Had it been correctly maintained; it would have run just as smoothly as the day it was made.

So, that was what he was chuntering at.

On the way down the stairs with his tea, she had heard him swearing, quickly followed by a barrage of tools clanking to the floor as if thrown in temper.

It had made her giggle, and in doing so, had spilt some of his tea.

"I'm sorry about the state of the cup. I'm afraid I spilt some on my way down."

"Oh, that's all right. I wouldn't have noticed if you hadn't mentioned it." He then took several long, satisfying gulps of the tea. "That's a grand cup of tea is that."

"It's my pleasure. I'm going to have a look around down here, so I'll leave you to it if you don't mind. If you need anything, just give me a shout."

"Will do." Then, placing his cup onto a nearby shelf, returned to his work.

After half an hour of genteel exploration through the rooms, offices, and the vast servants' hall – larger than any of the rooms upstairs, save for the conservatory – her search led her to the final door at the farthest end of the basement corridor.

Inside, she found old mops and buckets, dustpans and brushes, a nest of metal laundry tubs, cloths, carpet beaters, and a pile of scrubbing brushes. The shelves along the wall housed a vast assortment of soaps and cleaning supplies – everything necessary to keep a house of this size immaculately clean.

They had obviously forgotten about this room when the contents of the house had been cleared out back in the 1970s. But what an assortment of treasures for her to find!

This room had been frozen in time, untouched until she allowed the 21st century to seep into its depths.

She noticed paintings – large ones – leaning against the wall, their backs turned to the world. The housemaids must have brought them down to clean. And still, over a hundred years later, they waited.

She suddenly heard Mr Woodsman calling for her and immediately ran back to where he was working. "Is everything all right?" she asked, breathless.

His clean shirt, she noticed, was now covered with greasy, dark, smudged handprints, and smears. His sleeves were rolled up to his elbows, his forearms completely covered in slick, black grease.

"She's running like a dream now," he said with a satisfied smile.

"You're very clever to get it going again after all this time."

"Oh, it was nothing. All she needed was a bit of love and attention. These machines are so well built; they run themselves."

"Should I know how to operate it?"

"Oh, no," he laughed. "She's good to go for another hundred years or so now. I've set it all up for heat and hot water whenever you need it. I've checked the water filtration and ventilation systems. They needed a bit of a clean, but it's all systems go now – literally."

"Thank you. I'll be enjoying a much-wanted bath this evening, I think."

"Well, you'll have enough instant hot water to fill the village swimming pool," he laughed. "Is there anything else I can help with before I go?"

"Actually yes, there is."

She led him to where she had found the paintings.

After a closer inspection, Mr Woodsman noted signs of black mould creeping along the frames. If left untreated, it could spread to the rest of the house, posing both structural and health risks.

He suggested seeking a professional to assess whether the paintings could be salvaged but offered to take them down to the village in the meantime to prevent further contamination. In a little workspace above one of the shops, there was a wizened-looking old man that cleaned and restored old paintings. His fees were minimal as the old chap loved his work, and said it was more of a hobby than anything else.

She suggested making Mr Woodsman another cup of tea, which he gladly accepted as he set about carefully wrapping the paintings in several dust sheets he had brought from his van.

When she returned with his tea, he was about to wrap the final painting when he pointed out. "Look at this one." He propped the beautifully oval-shaped, gold-gilded framed painting as best as he could against the wall without it overbalancing. "If I didn't know any better, I'd swear blind this woman was you."

"Really?" she asked as she walked toward the painting, intrigued as she then bent to inspect it.

Through the wild brush strokes and tenacious pigments of the paints, the resemblance was indeed uncanny.

"You're right! If I didn't know any better, I'd think she was me too."

"The largest of the lot is almost entirely covered in mould. Of all of them, this ones in the best condition. But to be on the safe side – and if you don't mind – I'll include it with the rest. Mr Hardaker will be delighted when he gets his hands on these."

"I'm sure he will," Kathryn laughed. "I trust he's good at his job then?"

"Oh, yes. One of the best. Your paintings will be quite safe with him and finished to a faultless standard. So much so that they'll be returned to you like new. As though they'd just been painted yesterday shall we say."

"Oh, how exciting! How long will it take?"

"Typically, it takes a week or two per painting, depending on the extent of the damage. But from what I've seen, the only issue seems to be the mould, so the entire collection may take just a month or two to clean. As I said, he's very good at his work, or hobby, as he likes to call it."

"You sing his praises well."

"If I didn't, he'd have me hung, drawn, and quartered. He's my father-in-law, you see," he laughed. "But all that aside," he said seriously. "He really is very good, fastidious."

"I believe you," she laughed.

As she helped cover the painting with the dustsheet, she took one final look at the woman. It was like looking into a mirror. "The portrait of this woman looks as though it were painted on top of an original. Look, there's even paint on the inside of the frame where the portrait meets it."

"Well, would you look at that," he exclaimed. "My father-in-law's going to love this. Would you like this layer of paint removed? To reveal the original?"

"This woman was painted for a reason only the artist knew. So, for that reason, I'll leave it be. At least for now, anyway."

"As you wish."

∞ ∞ ∞

When the last of the paintings had been carefully loaded into the van, Kathryn became aware of the wistful chirps of unseen birds, their songs softened by the fog.

Then came another sound – shrill squeaks, or perhaps meows? She followed it around to the front of the van, where, on the passenger seat, a carry case sat secured by the safety belt. Inside, a cluster of contented little kittens huddled together in sleep, all but one, which looked up at her with an adorable little squeak.

"Oh my *gosh*! How beautiful!"

Mr Woodsman came and stood next to her and stared down at the mass of heaving fur with doting eyes. "I thought I'd call in on you on my way home from the vets. It was their three-month health check and vaccination today."

"Aww, bless them... Are they for sale?" she asked hopefully.

"I've just the one left still for sale, and that's the little girl staring up at us now. The only girl in the litter of four."

Kathryn was overjoyed.

She and Anna had begged their father for a pet, but he had always vehemently refused. He fulfilled their every want, need, and desire – they wanted for nothing. Yet, because of his severe allergy to animals, a pet had always been unequivocally out of the question.

"She's beautiful! They all are!"

Mr Woodsman reached into the carry case and lovingly cupped the kitten in his hands.

She was the most angelic thing Kathryn had ever seen, and her heart swelled with love already for this Heavenly tiny creature that now proudly belonged to her.

The kitten had the most delicate, heart-shaped face with lustrous jade eyes. And the biggest, pointiest ears Kathryn had ever seen a cat possess. Pale grey silken fur tipped with silver gave the kitten a shimmering, satin sheen.

"What breed are they?" she asked as she took hold of the kitten, which readily, and sweetly, meowed in almost answer to her question.

"Russian Blues."

"May I have her now?"

"I don't see why not," he replied as he ruffled the kitten's fur.

"Aww, look, sweetheart," Kathryn smiled as she turned to the house. "This is your house now. Welcome home, my little angel."

∞ ∞ ∞

After writing Mr Woodsman a cheque for his services and the kitten's procurement, Kathryn would set out for the village, determined to purchase food and a selection of essentials for her little darling. While there, she planned to introduce herself to the locals and extend an invitation to Lyon House for a Halloween party.

Surely, they would relish the chance to step inside after all this time. And perhaps, she could finally put an end to the superstition surrounding 'The Curse of Lyon House' – prove to them once and for all that it was simply a house, and people were merely people. They could look to her as proof – see how happy and healthy she was. She would call in on Mrs Carter also and invite her up to the house for afternoon tea.

"Come on now, my darling little sweetheart. Let's get you all warm and cosy on my bed. Mummy must go out and buy you lots of lovely things. Oh, just wait till I tell Aunty Anna about you!"

She sat on the bed, watching the kitten as it drifted into sleep.

As she did, a childhood memory surfaced – a book she had read long ago. In it, a rhyme spoke of animals and their 'true' names. If one wished to communicate fully with a creature, for both owner and pet to understand each other completely, one had to call it by its universally given name. And for the cat, that name was Ninkip. Ninkip, the cat.

Chapter 9

Kathryn sank into the deep, elegant, roll-top bath and sighed slowly in contentment as the hot water seemed to reach and warm her very essence. She lay with her eyes closed and listened to the song of the house – the pipes from running the hot water sang her a chorus of almost agonising wails and melodious moans, whilst the overflow chirped its tune as it sucked desperately at the water level every time she moved.

Ninkip lay asleep before the fire, embedded within the folds of Kathryn's bathrobe.

The fire was the bathroom's only source of illumination, and she watched sleepily as its flames ebbed and flowed their way up the chimney in long, lean licks.

She had left the bathroom door behind her ajar slightly to allow the steam to escape, though excess formed on the windows in front of her.

On the outside, feather light rain crystallised and began to skit, then scatter down the glass in an uninterrupted, haphazard way.

The fire crackled and hissed abruptly, bringing Ninkip from her slumber with a start.

"Oh, sweetheart. It's all right. It's only the fire."

Feeling soothed, Ninkip once again settled down within the safety of the bathrobe, during which, Kathryn began to sing Nat King Cole's rendition of 'Nature Boy'. She sang the ballad dolefully in a sweet soprano voice that tenderly held each note slowly, and lingeringly.

Her voice resounded hauntingly round the bathroom walls until it found its way out and down the corridor of the house.

She could see that Ninkip had responded to her singing, giving the occasional little squeak of appreciation.

So, continued with the song, but this time, humming it.

Suddenly, as if a huge gust of wind had taken ahold of the door, it flung itself open and slammed aggressively into the wall, causing Kathryn to swish round alarmingly in the bath.

She looked across at Ninkip, who was now sitting up alert, staring intently at the empty, open doorway.

Kathryn took slow, measured breaths, steadying her racing heart – for a moment, imagining the bathwater rippling in time with its frantic rhythm.

"Aww, my angel, it's all right. Come here, sweetheart." She offered her hand to the approaching Ninkip, who eagerly rubbed against it. "Silly Mummy must have left the bedroom window open."

She then closed her eyes and sank back down into the bath. And after one final prolonged, calming breath, reinstated to the end of the song, only this time, more woebegone than before.

Had she opened her eyes, she would have seen Ninkip frozen in place, pupils wide, fixated on something unseen – a presence that drifted soundlessly through the room, its shadow stretching where no shadow should be.

Chapter 10

Kathryn had laid out a medley of cakes and sandwiches on the coffee table in the drawing room in preparation for Mrs Carter's visit at three o'clock. The fire was burning brightly and spiritedly as it cavorted away. Ninkip was sleeping peacefully in front of it.

She followed Kathryn around the house like her little shadow. She even slept on the vacant pillow beside Kathryn in bed, refusing to set one tiny paw into the very plush, very costly cat bed.

Kathryn had never shared a bed with anyone, or anything before, so she found it entirely alien for the first few nights until she had got used to the presence of another living being.

On night's she was unable to sleep, she would watch Ninkip's little body rise and fall as she slept. How she doted on this fragile little cat that had unexpectedly entered her life, and, as a result, completed it.

She looked at the clock; it was a quarter to three. Mrs Carter would be here soon, so she set off to the kitchen to sort out the pot of tea and accompanying cups and saucers.

As she set them down onto the coffee table, she was startled by tapping on the window.

It was Mrs Carter.

Kathryn looked at the clock; it was just past three.

She ran up to the window and instructed Mrs Carter to meet her at the back door.

"Oh, my dear, I'm so sorry if I startled you," Mrs Carter said as Kathryn shut the door behind her. "I did knock, several times in fact, but you obviously didn't hear me."

"I'm so sorry. I was all the way down in the kitchen, making our tea. Can I take your coat?"

"Yes, thank you, dear." She took off her coat and handed it to Kathryn, who hung it on one of the hooks in the vestibule. "I'm *so* looking forward to a nice hot cup of tea. It's quite cold outside now. And the fog! How dreary it is. Don't you think, dear?"

"Oh, I don't mind the fog. In fact, I quite like it," she laughed. "It's been a never-ending overlay of fog for five days straight now since I moved in. Any excuse to get the fires lit and the lamps on. I think days like these are cosy," she smiled.

"Well, I'm glad *you* like it, dear. It's no good for my chest, though." She ended with a slight cough, adding momentum to her words.

"Come on through to the drawing room. It's delightful there, *and* warm. You can meet Ninkip too," she said excitedly.

As they walked into the drawing room, Mrs Carter gasped with joy. "Oh, my dear! I commend you on your style of furnishings! The place looks stunning!"

"Thank you. I'm so happy here. Beyond words in fact. Please, do sit down. Help yourself with sandwiches and cake. I'll be Mother and pour, shall I?"

"Oh, yes, thank you, dear. Oh, Kathryn, that must be Ninkip!" she sang out joyously after noticing the sleeping kitten before the fire. "What a tiny little thing she is. How has she accustomed herself to the size of the house? It is after all a huge haven for an animal to roam around in, is it not?"

"It is, yes, though she rarely strays far from me. Aside from feeding in the kitchen and using her litter tray, she's my constant companion."

"Aww, my dear. That's adorable."

"Do you have any pets?"

"I have two prized budgerigars named Jack and Jill," she laughed. "Poor Mr Carter can't stand them. He can't do with their constant chirping. And when I let them out of their cage for a fly about, off he goes to the pub to escape. I think he uses it as an excuse to go for a fleet-footed shandy. Bless him; I wouldn't have him any other way," she smiled.

"How long have you been married?"

"Fifty-two years now. Love at first sight for us both. We were married after only five weeks of meeting, and we haven't looked back since."

"How romantic," Kathryn exuded with a dreamy look about her face.

"Have you never married, dear?"

"No. I haven't been as fortunate as you and Mr Carter to have found my special one."

Living anyway, Kathryn mused as her thoughts went straight to Roman Lyons: Every evening before she went to bed, she would stare longingly up at him in the mural and would feel a wistful pang lurch in her stomach. And like a love-sick girl, would whisper to him a good night. Then every morning she would do the same, only wishing him a good day.

"Apart from my darling little Ninkip," she cooed. "She's Heaven-sent. I'm sure of it. Don't get me wrong; I've had a few boyfriends. But were all lacking the most important of attributes – they weren't my soulmate. Nothing less than that will do for me."

Time seemed to fly by as the two women sat chatting, lost entirely in each other's company. And, it would seem, a constant supply of tea.

When the clock sedately struck six, Mrs Carter looked flabbergasted.

"Oh, my word! Look at the time! I didn't realise quite how late it was. Mr Carter will wonder where I've got to. We sit down for dinner promptly at half-past-six every evening you know, dear. We old people and our routines shall never be broken," she finished with a laugh.

Kathryn smiled warmly at Mrs Carter as she hurriedly finished the remainder of her tea.

Mrs Carter seemed to be ruled by the time with a strict set of iron reins. Whereas she, Kathryn, hated the fact that we, as a whole, were governed and controlled by a manmade contraption known as the clock. It enchained us.

She hated the tedium of everything repeating in a constant cycle: Hours, days, weeks, months, and years, all repeated, and why? Who said? The clock was simply a fixture to keep us all complacent in life.

But *she* felt there was more. More to *her* life. And she knew deep down that somehow this house was the one variable that would knock off-kilter the cycle of which she so despised. She felt as though she had been lifted from the humdrum of reality, to live outside the restrictions of time and routine. To be only within the *welcome* constraints of Lyon House.

"Kathryn dear, I forgot to say. Your Halloween party is the talk of the village. We're all looking forward to it, enormously!" She clapped her hands together in exuberance.

"That's wonderful to know. I'm so pleased you told me. I had visions of my sitting alone in a room full of drying out food and evaporating drink!" she laughed.

"Oh, my dear, no! Everyone's running round like headless chickens trying to outdo one another with their costumes. It is a costume party, isn't it? I've been telling everyone that it is."

"It is. How will you be dressed?"

"Oh, my dear. That's a secret. You and the rest of the village will have to wait and see." She tapped the side of her nose a couple of times with her finger in a, 'I'm keeping it under wraps' way. "Where will it be?"

"I think the conservatory will be the perfect place, don't you? It has its own access too, so people won't be confused as to where to go."

"I think it's a sensational place to have it, dear. I can't wait!"

"Nor can I now I know I'll have actual guests," she laughed.

"My dear, you're getting the entire village!" Then, as an afterthought, she asked. "I know numerous party planners if you'd like their details, dear? Or perhaps the Myrtle Park Café?"

"Thank you, yes. I'll contact them immediately, seeing as I'll be feeding the five thousand."

Both women laughed as they walked down the corridor and into the vestibule to retrieve Mrs Carter's coat.

Once goodbyes had been issued, Kathryn returned to the drawing room and sat down onto the sofa.

One last piece of cake, I think. Then I must watch what I eat, or I will never fit into my dress for the party. Mrs Carter has been an evilly good influence of the indulgences of the amazing Café in the village. She would contact them and see if they would be available to cater for – it would seem – the entire village. Both she and Mrs Carter would be thrilled if they agreed to do the catering.

The sound of a dog barking interrupted her thoughts. It was coming from outside, at the front of the house.

I do wish that poor dog would find its way home. I'd help it if only I could see the thing!

Ninkip had not stirred, so the barking had fallen on deaf ears with her.

But there it was again, only further away now.

She assumed it to be a large dog, owing to its deep drawling tone. She hoped it would be all right; the cliff edge would be challenging to see in this fog, even for an animal.

She walked up to the window and peered out. Daylight had waned into dusk, bestowing the fog with a strange luminance. It was then that she noticed it – a large handprint on the glass. She frowned slightly as she placed her hand carefully onto it. It was not hers. It was much larger than her small hands. And besides, she would surely have remembered planting her hand in such a way on the windowpane. It was not something she would do.

It must belong to one of the removal men she thought as she pulled down her sleeve over her hand and began to clean the handprint unsuccessfully away.

So, assuming it to be the other side of the glass, she took a few serviettes from the now-abandoned tray of hers and Mrs Carter's tea, then bent down and kissed Ninkip on the head. "You stay here, my good girl. Watch for Mummy outside."

Ninkip responded with a light purr, then resumed her sleep.

Kathryn considered herself very lucky. Ninkip had the most *wonderful* of personalities – she was so loving and gentle, and not at all needy. She did not scratch the furniture, nor did she bite. She went to the toilet where she was supposed to. And the *most* incredible thing of all was, much to Kathryn's relief – she did not seem to like the outside world.

If Kathryn left a door or window open Ninkip would not venture outside. Instead, she would run away further into the house, usually to her favourite place – Kathryn's bedroom.

She was glad Ninkip seemed to have a fear of the outside. It kept her away from the cliff edge, and in doing so, kept Kathryn's fear of her falling from it well and truly at bay.

Kathryn ran from the house and all the way round to the drawing room window. She was eager to see Ninkip's reaction when she saw mummy from the other side of the glass. But no, Ninkip remained curled up tightly before the fire, utterly lost in her own warmth.

So, Kathryn rapped lightly on the window, but Ninkip's ears merely twitched. She was far too comfortable to move, even if it *were* to see her mummy peering in at her with wild excitement.

As Kathryn began to clean away the handprint on the glazing, it became apparent to her that it was unyielding.

Perhaps several sheets of glass had been pressed and fused together, encasing the maker's handprint within?

Mystified, she stepped closer to it and stared intently at it. She could see every line and swirl in accurate detail. It was a perfect impression.

She stepped back abruptly when she heard breaking glass from inside the drawing room.

She looked toward the fire – no sign of Ninkip.

Her heart lurched as she ran back around the house and finally inside. By the time she reached the drawing room, she was breathless.

"Ninkip?! Ninnie?" she tried to sound as calm as she could so as not to alarm the little kitten. "There you are."

Kathryn lightly ran towards Ninkip, who was inquisitively sniffing at something on the floor. She was in the bay window, in the same place that Kathryn had been standing trying to clean away that handprint.

Kathryn bent down and picked her up. "Don't drink that, my sweet. You don't know what it is."

Then she remembered the sound of breaking glass she had heard whilst outside.

There were no signs of injury to the kitten, and everything in the room was as it should have been, albeit a puddle of brown liquid on the floor by the window.

She looked up to the ceiling. No leaks. She looked to the window. No condensation. Nothing at all out of the ordinary, including broken glass.

She held Ninkip close to her, relieved all was well, and as the kitten's whiskers brushed against Kathryn's mouth, droplets of the liquid transferred onto her lips.

She pressed her lips together, tasting it.

This could not be.

She placed Ninkip down onto the sofa and returned to the liquid on the floor. She placed the serviettes that she still had onto the puddle and watched as it infused with the colours of the paper, giving it a distasteful brown tinge.

She picked up the now quenched serviettes, and with an investigative look, drew the scent to her nose. Brandy. It was brandy. She was certain of it.

How it got there, she could not explain.

She stood dazed for a while, clutching at the brandy-soaked serviettes, trying to find some sort of reasoning behind its appearance, when suddenly, again, the monster loud bark of that dog brought her out of her thoughts.

She looked to the window. But not through it. At it.

The handprint, she observed, was no longer there.

She stood back and looked at the large bay window in all its stately entirety... The handprint had gone.

"Perhaps Aunty Anna is right, Ninkip. Maybe I *should* get my eyes tested."

Chapter 11

Kathryn had returned home from the village satisfied that all plans for the Halloween party were well and truly underway.

The party was now only weeks away, so was approaching fast. She was eager to dress up, but the only thing that troubled her was little Ninkip – she would be frightened by all the unfamiliar people entering the house and the loud music Mrs Carter was organising. It was a local group, a band of musicians that played classical music.

She thought it was best for Ninkip to be in the office at the back of the house. It was one of the smaller rooms so would be safe and comfortable there. She would also make sure to provide some food and water, lots of playthings, and of course, her litter box.

She had spoken with Anna on the telephone, who had sounded well, but Kathryn could detect hints of sadness in her voice now and then, which of course, made *her* sad.

But they both had resigned themselves to the knowledge they would be reunited at the party. Anna had agreed to attend, due to the excitement of seeing Kathryn again. And as she had put it, 'the conservatory is quite far from the main body of the house, which is good. But I'll not be staying the night. I'll travel back home afterwards. It's only a two-hour drive.' Then, with more profound interest, had asked if she could do tarot card readings, with it being 'a Halloween party an all.' But before Anna's question was able to be completed, Kathryn had interrupted her with a firm, 'NO! Absolutely not,' which had finalised *that* topic of conversation. And of course, when Anna was presented with the announcement of a new family member – little Ninkip. She had nearly squealed with delight, prompting Kathryn to wince as she held the phone at arm's length, shielding her ear from an impending burst of sound.

She had felt a lightening of heart after speaking with Anna, and did not realise quite how much she had missed her. She was upset over Anna's refusal to stay the night. She had been hoping to spend some quality time together as they used to. Until Kathryn moved to Lyon House, they had been inseparable.

She loved her sister deeply, and once she was here at the house, she would do her very best to talk her into staying the night. And if she were to enjoy herself at the party, perhaps she would agree to stay a few days. Then Anna would see how happy and content she was, really see and understand her sense of belonging. Each day she would wake up happier than the day before, and always with a smile on her face.

∞ ∞ ∞

As night fell, Kathryn settled comfortably in the office with her laptop. She poured herself a generous glass of sweet white wine, sipping it steadily as she browsed various websites, selecting and purchasing books.

In truth, the sheer number of choices had been overwhelming, so in the end, she opted to purchase multiple 'job lots' of old classics. She hoped to find a few first editions among them but would have to wait patiently for their arrival. The thought of unpacking them all and filling the empty bookshelves in the library filled her with anticipation.

Oh, how dramatic it will be to once more *look* like the library it was intended to be! Every time she entered that room, she felt sad; she could almost feel its longing to be once again filled with knowledge.

She had found some old books in the local charity shops, but the amount she had was a tiny fraction of the massive volume she needed to be able to fill the library.

She leaned back in her chair, taking a few generous sips of wine. The taste was rich, comforting – perhaps a little too enticing.

Hours of staring at the laptop had left her drained. Her eyes felt dry and heavy, her limbs sluggish. But alongside the weight of exhaustion, the wine had begun to work its magic – a familiar warmth unfurling in her chest, lightening her thoughts even as her body grew heavier.

She closed her eyes to rest them and felt as though she were sunbathing on a peaceful beach, she could even feel the sea lapping at her feet. Had she looked down, she would have seen Ninkip making herself comfortable there.

Soon, the noise of the crackling fire became distant, and after that came the blackness of sleep.

When she awoke, the embers of the fire had collapsed to a dull red. And she was amazed and thankful to find that she still clung tightly onto the unspilled quarter glass of wine. She placed it carefully onto the desk and reached down to move Ninkip from her feet.

"Come on, Ninnie love, Mummy needs her feet back. Come on now. We both shall be more comfortable with you up on my lap."

Both Ninkip and she sat contentedly for a few moments before the music began.

It was the most beautiful, captivating, impassioned version of 'Songe d'Automne' she had ever heard. It hung on the air in meticulous strands of eminence – the moment the violin began, she was bewitched.

She sat unmoving in the chair, listening, unconcerned as to the whereabouts of its origins. Her entire body was enthralled by the musician who brought the wondrous music to life.

She closed her eyes and swayed gently with the rhythm, smiling. She wanted to get up and dance, she was moved to tears. Every hair on her body bristled, as if straining upward – reaching, yearning – to draw nearer to the bittersweet melody of this musical inferno, a firestorm that raged deep within her core.

She rose carefully from the chair, mindful not to disturb the sleeping kitten. Gently, she placed Ninkip into the warmth of her seat before leaving the office, drawn irresistibly toward the music that transfixed her.

The melody resonated in waves round the house, but as she entered the drawing room, the volume of sound surged sonorously.

She found herself observing her reflection in the bay window, and felt she was standing in the very root of which grabbed her.

She felt so alive, so happy, so carefree.

So... unafraid.

She set her arms as though holding onto the frame of a partner and danced. She whirled vivaciously and span sweetly about the room, all the while fantasising it was Roman Lyons that held her in his strong embrace.

Minutes passed in seconds, while seconds stretched into eternity. She felt as though she had stepped into another world – a dazzling, miraculous realm where she was utterly spellbound. The music held her captive, its notes weaving around her like whispers of an unspoken truth. She was caught within its pages, living within the musician's fingers, existing in perfect harmony with the piece. As she became entwined in its touch, nothing else remained. Only she – and it.

Faster and faster, she danced, spiraling into a dizzying state of bliss. Then, as if on cue, the music softened, fading into its inevitable diminuendo. With graceful ease, she descended to the floor, overcome by both joy and exhaustion.

Chapter 12

Kathryn settled into one of the plush chairs flanking the roaring fire in the library, a book resting in her hands – one of the pristine, timeworn volumes that had arrived a few days prior. Her online searches had unearthed a true treasure trove of classics, and, as she had hoped, several first editions were nestled among them. It had taken the better part of the day to arrange the books neatly onto the shelves, but now, at last, the library looked as it should – a space brimming with literary riches. It would take her years to work her way through them all, to finally exhaust the stories held within their pages.

She sighed deeply in contemplation as she placed her book down onto her lap.

Since her musical experience in the drawing room a week ago, more inexplicable occurrences had unsettled her.

The music and dance – those she could, at a stretch, attribute to the influence of alcohol. The sudden gusts of air rushing through the corridors, as if unseen forces were hastening past her – those, she reasoned, could simply be draughts from open windows.

But earlier today, when she had been standing looking out into the fog-ridden garden from one of the library windows, she had experienced a strange chill and tingling of her skin. Following that, she had felt the definite settle, then pull of something resting on her shoulder, like a firm grip of a hand. When she had turned around, there was quite obviously no one to be seen.

Through it all, she had never once felt afraid. Even her beloved Ninkip remained untroubled, showing none of the instinctive unease that animals display when something unseen and ominous lurks nearby. Like Kathryn, she seemed content, unfazed.

Even the unyielding fog – thick, ever-present – did nothing to dampen her thoughts or spirits. It was only a week until the end of October, and still, the fog had never lifted, not even for a few fleeting hours at midday when the sun reached its highest and burned its hottest.

She had also taken note of how it remained steadfast against the wind, holding firm as if it were iron-clad. It would always remain resolute, as though it were committed somehow in loyally guarding the house.

She even felt soothed on a night when in bed, listening to the doldrum moans of passing ships.

She felt at peace here, truly in unity with the place. She loved every second, every aspect of living here at Lyon House – her house.

She retrieved her book from her lap and resumed reading, once again dismissing the whispering voices around her as nothing more than the wind's restless murmur.

∞ ∞ ∞

Kathryn expected Mr Woodsman to arrive at any moment, excitement thrumming beneath her anticipation. He was bringing the painting of the woman – the one whose striking gaze had captivated her, whose features bore an unsettling, almost mirror-like resemblance to her own. Over the phone, he had mentioned that Mr Hardaker was thoroughly enjoying working on the pictures, but Kathryn could not shake the feeling that this particular portrait held something more – something inexplicably tied to her.

She fervently hoped Mr Woodsman would still come, despite the morning's unexpected snowfall.

That morning, upon drawing back the bedroom drapes, she had been startled to find snow falling thick and steady. Everywhere lay beneath a downy eiderdown of white. The fog, infused with an eerie, celestial brilliance, had dazzled her – almost blinding her as she gazed outside. It was then that she gauged the snow's depth to be at least a foot.

She had been told time and again by the locals – many of whom had lived there for generations – that snow was a rare occurrence. And even when it did fall, it never settled, the salt-laden air from the nearby sea ensuring it melted away. Bingley was a small, picturesque village perched on the edge of the East Yorkshire coast, cradled between the vast, rolling countryside and the endless expanse of the deep blue sea.

So, she thought, this must feel surreal to them all – waking up to such an unexpected sight. But to her, it was a deep comfort. She adored snow with the same fervour she had for fog, so its presence was of little consequence to her.

She had always loved nature's wild extremes – thick fog, heavy snow, wicked thunderstorms, torrential rain, and howling winds. Perhaps that made her rather dull, she mused with a smile. Yet, the house seemed intent on granting her every silent wish, fulfilling her unspoken desires like a guardian watching over her.

If only it would give her the Master of the house himself – one Roman Lyons. Now, *that* would be something!

The high reverberating sound of a struggling van became audible, so she peered out of the window. She had been seated in the grand hall for some moments now awaiting the arrival of Mr Woodsman.

She was sure this would be him as she was expecting no other.

Then came the steady sound of a door slide open then closed immediately afterwards.

Time seemed to idle away as she waited, and still, she could see no man, nor movement through the bank of snowy fog. Then suddenly, there he was, standing before the porch as though he had just stepped out from another world entirely.

Her heart leapt with joy as she rushed away from the window to greet him at the door.

"Mr Woodsman, I'm so pleased you're here! I was afraid you wouldn't make it what with the weather being how it is."

"I nearly didn't make it," he replied as she closed the heavy, cumbersome doors behind him. "It's not *half* as bad as this in the village." He put down his tool bag, then carefully placed the painting on the floor beside the wall. "Mr Hardaker insisted I couldn't take it from his workshop until he'd securely wrapped it."

She looked at the package.

If he had spent this much time, care, attention, and consideration on the wrapping of it, then she was sure that the actual painting would be of a supreme standard also.

He had swathed it in thick brown paper, and the wrapping of it only a professional gift-wrapper in department stores would be envious. He even had secured all jaunty angles of it with twine and finished it with a neatly tied double bow. It would not have looked amiss if it were placed underneath a gallant Christmas tree. Indeed, it would be the most eye-catching of all the shrouded gifts.

"Where would you like to have the unveiling? I've brought my drill in case you'd like me to mount it on the wall for you."

"Have you not seen it yet?"

"Me?!" He laughed heartily. "Nope. Mr Hardaker refuses anyone entry into his workshop, even his wife isn't allowed in."

"Really?" she laughed.

"Really. He has his own ways and funny little eccentricities when it comes to him and his work," he laughed.

"Each to their own," laughed Kathryn. "I think we'll have the unveiling in the office. I'd like to see it mounted on the wall above the fireplace. It'll finish that unoccupied area off beautifully."

Once in the office, she unwrapped it with careful precision. It would have been unjust to have simply ripped it open after Mr Hardaker had spent his time painstakingly wrapping it to such high quality.

Plus, she wanted to make the occasion linger; this was, after all, a gift from the house.

"Look, Mr Hardaker added a hanging chain, so we can place it directly on the picture rail. Let's hang it first, then remove the last protective card covering the woman – so we get the best first view. What do you think?"

"I think, let's do it!" It took only moments for him to hang the painting. "There you go. Over to you."

She carefully peeled off the remaining card that was lightly adhered to the frame.

Then, they stood back and stared in awe.

The portrait hung dignified and snugly, dead centre of the chimney breast.

The painting's insipid colours lent it a misty, almost spectral appearance, while the baroque frame – gilded in brilliant 22k gold – exuded the opulence favoured by the wealthy. The stark contrast between the painting and its frame was striking, yet together, they were undeniably resplendent.

"It's beautiful," Kathryn said. "It's like it was meant to be – hanging it there. I can't wait to see the others," she beamed.

Mr Woodsman remained silent. He could not tear his attention away from the picture, it held him in the form of suspended animation.

As with most occupants of portraits, their eyes would keenly follow your every move. But with this one, its stare was most direct, almost blank. As if the woman in the painting were lifeless and staring at absolutely nothing at all. The positioning of the head looked as though she had just turned around quickly in shock, her long hair caught in frozen momentum as it made to swirl about her neck and shoulders.

"You know," he mused. "When you look at the woman, really *see* her I mean. Her hair. Can you see? Even her hair's like yours. They didn't have fringes in Victorian times, did they? And they always had it tied up, styled and neat."

"I'm not sure," she pondered as she leaned in to inspect the woman closely. "I didn't realise you had such a vast knowledge of Victorian ladies' hair styles," she laughed mischievously.

"I must admit," he said as he turned to face her. "My knowledge *does* come from the period films my wife loves to watch. The parts I'm not asleep for anyway," he finished with a laugh.

"Well, there you go then," she laughed. "That's *that* little notion quenched. Plus, how do we know it *is* from that time? There's no date or signature, so it could be more modern than we think."

But deep down, she did indeed agree with everything Mr Woodsman had just presented to her. Her own father if he were here today alive and well, would swear emphatically that the woman in the painting was her – regardless of eras, dates, and fashions. And that is why she had deduced irrefutably against showing Anna this portrait. For if she *were* to see it, it would become just another motive on top of the many others Anna had for her to leave this 'death house' as she had christened it. And she did not want to give her any more reasons to never return to Lyon House. If anything, she wanted desperately to provide Anna with motivation to *stay*, if only for a few days at least after the Halloween party.

"I'm looking forward to meeting your wife. We have a common interest already – period films. And now, since moving here, well, I feel I've immersed myself in my very own period saga," she laughed.

"My wife's on cloud nine about the Halloween party. If I'm not mistaken, she's organised for us to be dressed in period costume – her as Lady of the Manor, and me, the lowly gamekeeper, of course," he laughed.

"That's brilliant!" she laughed gleefully. "I can't wait to see what everyone will arrive as. We'll be like characters from our very own book."

"What are you wearing?"

"Surely you can guess." She gave him a few moments, and when no answer was forthcoming. "A Victorian lady, naturally," she responded with a laugh.

"Very fitting! It's been a long time since Lyon House has had a Victorian Lady wander its halls."

"Well, I only hope I can do the dress justice. It's been hanging in the wardrobe for days now. I've resisted the urge to wear it. But now the temptation is becoming overwhelming. But I won't give in. I want to savour the moment and wait patiently for Halloween."

"Which is only a few days away. I hope this weather improves or I'm afraid you may have to cancel. No one will be able to get here. I only made it today by the skin of my teeth."

"Skin of my teeth," she repeated. "I've never heard that saying before," she laughed.

"It's a fond one of the wife's," he chuckled. "She's a character."

"Well, I'll be positive when I say that I'll look forward to meeting her at the party."

"I'll keep my fingers crossed for you. Speaking of which, you must cross them for *me*. I need to be getting back home now; she'll be clock-watching and worrying."

"Of course. They're crossed. See." She held up her hands to show her conviction. "I'll walk you out."

Chapter 13

The darkness seemed to fall heavily on the night of Halloween. And much to Kathryn's relief, the snow had cleared entirely. The only persistent remnant to bear witness of the snow ever having been there at all, was frost. It clung unrepentantly to everything it touched.

The conservatory held within it a hive of activity as preparation remained underway for the party later that evening.

Excitement surrendered her impatient to see inside, but she had entrusted the party planners and caterers implicitly with all decisions concerning the food and decorations. All she had asked was for everything to be graceful and stylish.

She had got Ninkip settled in the office. So now, all that had to be done was to dress for the evening. The guests were due to arrive within the hour, so that gave her sufficient time to prepare herself.

She wore her make-up simply, subtly enhancing her eyes, cheeks, and lips, just as ladies would have done in the Victorian era. And for her hairstyle, two unadorned clips – one placed and secured either side of her head ensured her hair fell in a waterfall of loose, cascading curls – although not how the ladies back then would have worn it, but she wanted a more 'present merging with the past' look for the party.

Her gown was a Victorian black bodice dress, adorned with a jacquard brocade print. She wished Anna were here to help – fastening the bodice would be a challenge, but she would have to manage as best she could and hope it would suffice.

She could not wait to see Anna and introduce her to her beloved little Ninkip. She would fall instantly in love with her, just like she herself had done a mere month ago. Now she could not imagine life without Ninkip; she could not imagine life *before* Ninkip. She loved her so very; very much.

She removed the outfit and all its accessories from out of the wardrobe and placed everything carefully onto the bed. She did not realise quite how cumbersome the 6-hoop skirt was, so reasoned the best course of action was to be the footwear first – a pair of black leather lace-up Victorian boots, complete with nailhead heels.

How fancy they were! It was such a shame that no one would see them underneath her dress.

She layered the black wide-sweep underskirt first, then the overskirt. Lifting the fabric eyelet loops, she secured them around the button facets at each hip, cinching the overskirt to reveal the underskirt beneath. The gathered effect gave the dress a refined elegance.

She adored the way the material whispered under her touch as she smoothed it into place – and oh, how it swished delightfully when she moved!

She was only half-dressed, and yet already she felt she had taken on the part of a real-life Victorian Lady.

Lastly, the bodice – the long sleeves fit her arms so perfectly; it was as though they had been delicately painted on. They feathered out to her knuckles in a detailed pattern of lace. She also managed to pull and tie the lace-up detailing at her back, ensuring the snuggest of fits.

And finally, to complete the look – a matching black choker of lace and brocade gave the illusion of the bodice to be high-necked.

She gazed at the mirror in awe, feeling entrancing – beautiful in a way that transcended time. It was like seeing a character from a beloved historical novel come to life before her eyes. It wasn't about being a man or a woman; the true allure lay in embodying the past itself. And it was precisely because she was wrapped in history that she became mesmerising – captivating in a way only time could grant and bestow.

She could even feel how her posture had changed. She was carrying herself differently, correctly. And by the time she had reached the conservatory, she *did* feel as though she were a Victorian Lady from a novel of days gone by.

The conservatory was a breathtaking spectacle. The party planners had truly outdone themselves.

Illuminated pumpkins served as the primary light source – flickering flames encased within, scattered generously throughout the room. Others were suspended at dizzying heights, hanging seemingly at random from the ceiling. Invisible wires created the uncanny illusion that they drifted freely, as if possessed. Together, they merged into a mass of haunting brilliance – the perfect glow of Hell itself.

A collection of trees of varying sizes had been brought in, their leaves stripped away, left stark and bare. Their only adornment – a cloak of artificial crows, clustering majestically on the branches in a shimmering fabric of iridescent black. Nestled within their plumage, hints of green and purple gleamed like spectral embers.

Ornate mirrors of various shapes and sizes had been painted black, their surfaces disrupted by swirling tendrils of white paint – agitated to create the illusion of billowing smoke. To the brave souls who dared to gaze into the 'Mirror of Captured Souls,' a chilling vision awaited – a distorted, terrifying interpretation of the spirit imprisoned within.

Lastly, enormous urn-style vases were filled with an array of orange and black flowers.

There were four sizable tables, each filled with a different selection of food.

The first display featured an assortment of dips served in test tubes and science beakers. Crudités were carefully carved into the form of a Day of the Dead skeleton, while tortilla chips, shaped like gravestones, stood alongside devilled eggs and cauldrons overflowing with crisps.

Cheese and crackers completed the spread, with the cheese sculpted into every Halloween-themed shape imaginable – bats, spiders, ghosts, cats, witches, and pumpkins. And finally, stuffed mushrooms transformed into squidgy eyeballs, their hidden gooey cheese spilling messily down the chins of all who dared take a bite.

The second table had pizzas, decorated to look like spiderwebs. Ghost shaped sandwiches, and baguettes were cut, shaped and designed in such a way as to resemble coffins, with the occupant being the sandwich filler.

Adorning the third table were toffee apples, pumpkin pie, sugar skull cookies, buns, and doughnuts sporting terrifying faces. A giant spider cake, its multitude of glistening beady eyes unnervingly lifelike, sat alongside a life-sized pumpkin cake. But Kathryn's favourite was the masterpiece – a grand, towering cake depicting Lyon House in stunning detail.

Lastly, the fourth and final table, a choice of alcoholic and non-alcoholic beverages, all served in vintage jam jars.

A smaller table provided a range of old-fashioned floral plates and cutlery, complete with matching napkins.

The Myrtle Park Café had accomplished something truly impressive. She was glad she had resisted the temptation – more than once throughout the day – to sneak a peek inside. Had she given in, she would not have been met with this breathtaking scene in its full, spectacular glory. Seeing it now as a complete vision was far more satisfying than glimpsing it in fragments.

A mishmash of sound began as each musician tuned their instrument to match the oboist A440. The orchestra was to play classical music throughout the night, with requests from guests to be obliged.

Now it was time for Kathryn to take her place at the door to greet her guests. The fog was thicker than ever this evening, but she could just make out the bustling sounds of the first of many guests drawing near. They all chatted and laughed eagerly in suspense of their evening ahead.

For over an hour, she had stood steadfast in the doorway, acquainting herself with witches and warlocks, cowboys and outlaws. Zombies, werewolves, vampires, and mermaids. Doctors and nurses, Disney characters, phantoms, fairies, kings and queens. Animals, skeletons, pirates, superheroes and villains, historical figures. Even the Grim Reaper himself. The sheer variety of costumes was astonishing, a dazzling display of creativity. Someone had even arrived as Santa Claus!

"Lady Chatterley and her lowly gamekeeper lover, I presume?" Kathryn greeted.

"How'd you guess," replied Mr Woodsman with a laugh. "This is the wife – Lady Chatterley."

"Very pleased to meet you, Milady," Kathryn laughed. "You both look incredible."

"Aww, thank you; so do you. Your dress is gorgeous," said Mrs Woodsman. "Thanks so much for inviting us. I've been looking forward to this evening so much that I've been wishing away the days," she laughed.

"Well, no more wishing your days away. Please, do go in and help yourself to food and drink."

As 'Lady Chatterley' entered the conservatory, Kathryn smiled and turned to Mr Woodsman, asking who the quiet elderly couple who stood slightly behind him were. "And who do we have here?"

"Here we have Einstein himself, accompanied by his lovely wife. Also known as my in-laws," he laughed.

"Oh, Mr Hardaker! It's such a pleasure to meet you at last."

Mr Hardaker had stood in silence as he watched his daughter and son-in-law chat merrily away to Kathryn White. And now, now her eyes were upon *him*, he felt as though Medusa herself had turned him into stone.

"Are you all right? You look as though you've just seen a ghost." Kathryn looked about the conservatory and laughed. "A *real* one at that... Mr Hardaker?"

"*You're her*," he replied astounded after finally finding his voice. "*The woman from the paintings!*"

Kathryn laughed nonchalantly. "The resemblance is quite beyond belief, isn't it."

"This can't be," he said dumbfounded.

"What? What can't be Mr Hardaker?"

"*You*."

Kathryn frowned at Mr Woodsman, concerned. And as she drew breath to speak, a loud strident voice prevented her.

"Kathryn! Dear! You look out of this world!" Mrs Carter exclaimed as she appeared from out of the fog.

"Please, do go on inside. It's getting cold out here," Kathryn said kindly as she ushered Mr Woodsman and the Hardaker's inside. "Mrs Carter," she smiled. "Look at you. You're positively alluring."

Everyone had made an arresting effort. But Mrs Carter had, in Kathryn's opinion, stolen the show. She looked both elementary and exquisite, wearing only a shawl of cheesecloth wrapped around her body that fell unfetteredly to the floor. Attached to it, there were a few dozen large fake spiders. She had even placed one in her hair that fell naturally onto her shoulders. Underneath the shawl, ensuring her dignity remained, she wore a flesh-coloured swimsuit. Her figure, thought Kathryn, put all the young girls to shame. Including herself.

"Oh, Kathryn, just listen to that beautiful music! They're playing 'Emperor Waltz' – how lovely. Do you know how to waltz, dear?"

"Of course."

"Come along then; I'll lead."

"I should really stay here, in case any more guests arrive."

"Kathryn, you're freezing, and I will be too if I stay out here any longer in this outfit." Her eyes roamed around the conservatory. "The turnout is most admirable, my dear. From the looks of it, all the village is already inside, and we're the only two who aren't. It looks like a wonderful party, so let's go and be a part of it. If anyone else *does* arrive, it won't be the end of the world that you're not here to greet them. And I'm sure they're more than capable of opening a door and coming in."

Kathryn nodded her head in agreement. "To be honest, I've been *aching* to get inside and have a dance," she replied as she shut the doors to the conservatory.

Kathryn grasped Mrs Carter's hand and followed her into the crowd of dancers.

They chatted happily together as they progressed about the room dexterously with unwavering balance and decorum. All the while with Mrs Carter enlightening her about beliefs and customs of the Victorians during the festivities of Halloween.

One of which was more Anna's idea of awe than hers, but still interesting nonetheless, was a tale of veils between worlds.

According to Mrs Carter, it is said that on Halloween, the veil between the earth and the spirit world is at its thinnest – sometimes lifting, if only for a moment, allowing the two realms to merge.

She had also said that like February 14th, October 31st was *also* revered for its potency in the proclamation of finding new love, or indeed, the promise of it.

"You dance very well, Kathryn dear. I've been a dancer all my life and can tell the instant I hold someone if they're to be any good. And you, Kathryn, are sublime. Most proficient."

"I must give my dad all the credit. He taught Anna and me from a very early age."

"He must have been very good."

"Oh, he was. To be honest, there wasn't anything that my dad couldn't do well."

"Your father and I would've gotten on famously. Where is Anna tonight, my dear? She is coming, isn't she?"

"I hope so. She promised me faithfully that she'd be here. I shan't worry just yet; I'm assuming she's running late."

"Well, I hope she arrives soon, the evenings nearly half gone."

"I know," she replied sadly. "I don't want it to end."

"All good things, Kathryn my dear. All good things. And speaking of, let's go and get some of that delicious-looking food before it's all gone."

"I am famished. I haven't eaten anything all day, what with the excitement of tonight."

"Kathryn dear, you must eat. You'll wilt away otherwise." She took hold of Kathryn's hand and pulled her gently towards the table that contained the desserts. "I must say, Myrtle Park Café has done a monumental job, haven't they?"

"They have. I left all the decision making entirely to them. When I walked in here this evening and saw everything for the first time it took my breath away."

"I anticipated nothing less from everyone who organised tonight's event. Kathryn, let's sample one of these toffee apples."

Kathryn watched as Mrs Carter crunched her way through the hard, amber glassy surface and through to the soft, sympathetic apple.

"Not for me, thank you. I don't think my poor teeth could stand up to that," she laughed.

"Wait till you get to my age, Kathryn dear. You can eat *anything*. False you know," she replied before taking another rapturous bite.

Rather than indulging too much, Kathryn opted to nibble at one of the last remaining sugar skull cookies. But soon, she knew she would not be able to resist the spiderweb pizza – it looked simply too tempting.

"Excuse me, Miss White?"

Kathryn turned around from the table to see a young, well-presented looking girl, smiling inquiringly at her.

One of the party planners she assumed. "Yes?" she replied with a smile.

"When would you like the game of 'Oranges and Lemons' to begin?"

"I'd forgot about that. You can announce it after the orchestra's finished playing this piece."

"Kathryn dear," Mrs Carter politely interrupted. "I'm just going to get a drink. Would you like one?"

"That would be lovely, thank you. I'll have some of that blue-coloured drink please."

"That's the one I'm going to have too! It looks very engaging, doesn't it? Let's hope it tastes it too," she finished with a laugh.

"And the announcement for the most outstanding and original costume?" the party planner asked after Mrs Carter had danced nimbly away for the drinks.

"After the game I think – while we have everyone's attention."

"Are you going to take part?"

"I'd love to, but I'd better not. Can you imagine if I won? Everyone would think it was fixed," she laughed lightheartedly.

"A wise choice," laughed the party planner. "Now, if you'll excuse me, I'll inform the orchestra. It'll be a welcome break for them, I'm sure."

"Please tell them to help themselves to food and drink, will you?"

"I will."

Before Kathryn could reach for that wondrous slice of pizza, Mrs Carter came hurriedly towards her, almost spilling the drinks that she was holding.

"Kathryn dear," she spluttered out as she thrust one of the drinks into Kathryn's hand. "What on earth have you done to Mr Hardaker? I've just seen him leaving, with his poor wife having to hold him up! He looked as grey as a cemetery headstone. I could hear him incoherently referring to you in a painting that he's currently working on that's over a hundred years old."

"Poor Mr Hardaker. I'm sorry I gave him a shock. I should've realised with him never having met me until tonight. You see, he's been working on some paintings I found in the basement. They were in quite a state, so Mr Woodsman gave them to him to work his magic on. One of which, I must admit, could quite easily be mistaken for me. It must be that of which he's referring. I'll show you if you'd like? Unless of course, you'd prefer to stay for a game of 'Oranges and Lemons'? It's due to start any moment."

"Heavens no," Mrs Carter laughed. "'Oranges and Lemons' indeed! I'd rather go with you and see this painting that's got poor Mr Hardaker all of a fluster. Though, he did seem *very* insistent on it being his *current* painting." She paused, deep in thought. "But then again, he *was* knocking back quite a few drinks," she finished with a playful giggle.

"Mrs Carter, you *are* terrible," she replied, humorously. "I hope he's going to be all right."

"Never mind about him, dear. All *I'm* interested in now is this painting of yours. How thrilling," she laughed.

∞ ∞ ∞

"My dear! No wonder the poor chap was so discombobulated! Although it's quite impossible, I would *still* state my life and worth on this woman, this portrait, being you."

"It's quite extraordinary, isn't it?"

"I don't think extraordinary is quite the word for it, dear. I think incomprehensible would be better suited for it."

"Do you think so?"

"Yes. Yes, I do. The same hair." She looked back and forth between the picture and Kathryn, examining them both in detail. "You even have the same eyes. It's uncanny. And slightly unnerving."

"Unnerving?"

"Yes. How strange to think that the woman in this painting is you – or rather, *looks* like you. We've already determined that it's impossible for her to *be* you, and yet... the resemblance is unnerving. It's as if the past has cast its reflection forward in time, a ghostly imprint of something yet to come."

"How much alcohol did *you* consume whilst eavesdropping on poor Mr Hardaker's theories?" Kathryn laughed.

"Not enough. Evidently," she chuckled.

"You know what I think."

"What's that, my dear?"

"I think you and Mr Hardaker have very vivid imaginations."

"Perhaps you're right. I must investigate Lyon House further. See if I can turn up anything else."

"There you go. Rational actions born from rational thinking will always lead to rational answers." Kathryn nodded in quiet agreement with herself.

"Yes, I suppose so."

"Now then, speaking of rational answers. Can you tell me if anyone in the village has lost a dog? A large one at that. I keep hearing it barking in the grounds. I've never seen it. It always seems to stay far enough away from the house. But then again, it could be as close as we are to each other now and I wouldn't see it in this fog."

She glanced toward the window, watching as Ninkip paced back and forth along the sill, her gaze fixed outside. It was as if she were tracking something unseen.

"Aww, what is it, my love?" she murmured, crossing over to the kitten and stroking her gently. "I can't see anything, Ninnie... but I can hear it."

She turned to Mrs Carter. "Can you hear it?"

"Hear what, dear?"

"Shouting. A man, I think. He's shouting at his dog. Can't you hear it barking? It's not very loud, but most distinctive all the same. Just look at Ninkip. She can hear it quite clearly. *And* see something. There's definitely something outside. Though for the life of me I can't see anything but fog."

She bent forward and leaned closer to Ninkip in the hopes she could see what the kitten could. Then, abruptly, the window opened with a sudden whoosh, causing Kathryn to step back quickly in shock, and as if by a pair of unseen hands, Ninkip was pushed outside.

"*OH MY GOD!!*" Kathryn shouted horrified as she watched Ninkip disappear into the fog.

"Kathryn, what is it?!" Mrs Carter asked in fright.

"*Somethings just pushed Ninkip out of the window!*"

"What?!"

"*NINKIP'S GONE!*" she shouted hysterically as she ran out of the office.

Chapter 14

Mrs Carter had sat tentatively waiting in the office for Kathryn's return with little Ninkip, so when the figure of a man stepped into the room, she was both disappointed, and disconcerted.

"Hello, Mrs Carter. How are you?"

"Anna? Is that you?" She stood up from the chair in amazement. "Oh, my goodness me. It *is* you!" she laughed. "You look unbelievable! You and your sister make quite the pair! I wouldn't have known. Your voice, dear, that was the only giveaway. What a fine Victorian Gentleman you make. And that moustache! How real it looks!"

"I've a friend that's training to be a special effects make-up artist. So, I was her practice piece for tonight. She's done that well I don't recognise even myself when I look in the mirror," she laughed. "That's why I'm late, you see, I wanted to surprise Kathryn. No doubt she expects me to arrive as a gypsy, crystal ball in hand. How shocked she'll be," she laughed. "Where is she? I couldn't find her in the conservatory."

∞ ∞ ∞

Kathryn's heartbeat was deafening as she ran frantically through the forbidding concealment of fog and around to where she had seen Ninkip swallowed into obscurity.

A sharp splinter of light pierced the fog from the office window, illuminating wisps and tendrils that seemed to claw desperately at the darkness, yearning to break through.

In the office, she could see Mrs Carter talking to a man – she wished she too were in its warmth and light with Ninkip by her side, safe and sound.

From behind her, she felt the slight movement of something push up against her dress. "Ninkip?" she whispered as she turned away from the window. "Is that you? Come here, my angel. It's all right. Don't be afraid."

She stumbled through the murk until she reached the pond. There, motionless against the wall, crouched Ninkip. She looked at Kathryn – her eyes huge, round, black, and filled with fear.

A small line of fur had sprung up along the length of her arched back, and her tail had doubled its thickness to form a bushy mass that she had tucked between her legs in confusion.

Kathryn's eyes welled with stinging tears as she scooped Ninkip into the warmth and safety of her arms. Holding her tightly against her chest, she gently sang the lullaby 'Hush, Little Baby,' her soft voice a soothing balm for the frightened kitten.

As Ninkip began to purr, a low, deep growl rumbled from behind Kathryn. A slow wave of terror crept over her, rising from her feet to her head, wrapping her in its chilling grasp.

She turned slowly, afraid of what she would be faced with.

But there was nothing - nothing that she could see. Only the sound. The sound of fear itself, raw and unfiltered in its purest form.

Her nose prickled with terror – but not for herself, for Ninkip. Her beloved, beautiful little darling, the precious soul she adored with every fibre of her being. She would protect her with her life.

As vicious barks joined the growls, she clutched Ninkip tighter, pressing her closer to her chest.

Ninkip was still purring. That was good. So, Kathryn continued to sing. Each note an octane of trepidation.

She continued to sing when quick sporadic blasts of heat and droplets of horror splashed upon her face.

She continued to sing through each deafening snarl of rage as it sucked her heart further up into her throat.

She continued to sing as Ninkip looked up at her trustingly with eyes full of love.

She continued to sing as tears warmed her cold face.

And still, she sang – her voice unwavering even as the massive hellhound burst from the fog, its brute force slamming into her shoulders, sending her and Ninkip hurtling backward toward the pond.

As she fell, the world twisted in slow motion, and through the suffocating fog, a man's voice thundered – "*Ferret!!*"

∞ ∞ ∞

The pond's icy armour lay firm and strong, protecting its soft underbelly.

All but one slice remained, as if a portion had been taken out like a piece of pie. There, it was split into deathly sharp shards as though something, or someone, had broken through and disappeared beneath.

An icy scar already began its formation on the still trembling surface, busily knitting all the pieces back together, as if in eagerness to cover up a terrible misdeed.

Anna sank beside the pond and sobbed so heartwrenchingly, the angels themselves looked down upon her with sadness, and cried.

Part Two

Roman Lyons

Chapter 15

The sound of thundering hooves proclaimed the imminent, and subsequent return, of one, Master Roman Lyons. A magnificent, sleek, grey, Great Dane gambolled dutifully along beside his Master, clutching tightly within his almighty jaws a bright yellow ball.

Mrs March awaited her Master with avid eyes as green and lush as rich, vibrant lurid grass. And with hair the colour of a newly turned autumn red leaf, one could say she had been put together uncommonly well. As if Mother Nature herself had played a part in her being.

She tightened the belt that secured her matronly figure, setting the keys suspended from her chatelaine jangling in a metallic chorus.

Beside her stood her husband, dressed in his khaki best – the perfect attire for the head gardener. And finally, Miss Leighton, the housemaid, whom she gestured toward, prompting her to straighten her askew cap at once.

Mrs March smoothed down her plain yet elegant black dress and lifted her head high, a smile forming as she watched the great white stallion approach, her Master astride.

As she stood here today, watching him approach, her mind drifted back to the last time she had seen him – twenty-eight years ago, when he had been just ten. What a beautiful, sensitive, delicate child he had been. If she had to choose only one word to describe him, it would be 'Heavenly.'

With eyes as bright as the clearest blue sky and hair as dark as an inky black night, he had been nothing short of angelic. And with a temperament to match, he was, without question, the most perfect child she had ever laid eyes upon.

It was at the insistence of the then Master that Roman be sent away to receive the finest education that only life abroad could provide. But being the sensitive little soul he was, he had cried and sobbed so wretchedly, clinging to the Mistress with such desperation that he had to be physically pried from her embrace.

For months afterward, the memory haunted the Mistress, forcing the doctor to visit daily – prescribing tonics for sleep, then tonics for waking. Yet the Master remained resolute, declaring that it would make a man of the boy, teach him the ways of the world.

But beneath the household's unspoken thoughts, they all knew the true reason he had been sent away – to ensure that Lyon House would forget him.

The man who dismounted jauntily from the horse was no longer angelic – he had transcended all Heavenly beings and risen to the stature of a god. Broad-shouldered and wide of smile, had his garments been draped over one of the sublimely carved statues in the conservatory, one might have mistaken it for the very form of Roman Lyons himself.

She glanced at Miss Leighton and was dismayed to see her blushing – she would have to keep a watchful eye on her. Miss Leighton could be flighty at the best of times, but such behavior in front of the Master was wholly improper. No housemaid, least of all one in her position, should conduct herself in such a manner.

"I fear I've brought the fog with me – it's been snapping at my heels ever since I set foot on the Coach Road. If I weren't of sound mind, I'd swear it was chasing me!" he laughed, his voice rich with amusement.

"Welcome home, sir," Mrs March said with a graceful curtsey.

"Mrs March?! This cannot be! How is it that you remain as young and radiant as when I saw you last? Look at you – you confound me. Not a single thread of grey woven through your hair, not the slightest change. Truly, it defies reason."

She met his gaze with a knowing smile. "I see you've been well educated in flattery, sir," she replied, her tone tinged with quiet authority.

"Indeed, I have," he laughed. "And, Mr March! How are you, my good man?"

"I'm doing very well, thank you, sir."

"And this is?" He looked down at Miss Leighton, who could not control an escaping giggle. He looked to Mrs March with a questioning gleam in his eye.

"I'm sorry, sir. This is Miss Leighton – the housemaid."

"Miss Leighton," he acknowledged with a bow of his head. Then turning back to Mrs March. "I hope you won't take this as undue criticism, but I rather expected a larger gathering to welcome me upon my arrival."

"We're the only staff. But don't fret – you'll find the house in pristine order."

"Indeed, I have no doubt. You always did have a place for everything, and everything in its place."

"And very proud of that she is too, sir," Mr March quipped in with a smile. "I'll take the horse round to the stables."

"Thank you, Mr March."

As they watched the horse's swishing tail disappear into the fog, the sound of muffled barking began.

"Ferret! Come!" Roman called.

"Ferret?" Mrs March asked.

"Yes," he laughed. "It is rather an odd name for such a large animal, but, owing to him resembling one at birth, I felt it my duty to name him as such."

The Great Dane galloped obediently to his Master's side, dropped the ball from his mouth, and sat down beside him.

"I trust my belongings have arrived safely?"

"Yes, sir. Yesterday."

"Very good." He turned and looked at the house. "It seems far smaller than I remember."

"Things usually do when you've been away for as long as you have. To leave a place as a child as you did, then return an adult, you see things from a different perspective."

"How wise you are."

"It's such a pleasure having you home, sir. But if only the circumstance were of a happy nature."

"Come now, let's not dwell on the past. It won't do us any good." He picked up the ball that lay at his feet and threw it to the other side of the courtyard.

Ferret went hurtling after it at his Master's command of 'fetch', and within minutes had brought it back and dropped it once again before Roman. He then wandered over to the pond and sniffed round it searchingly before finding the perfect place to drink. He drank eagerly, intrigued by the ripples he made.

Roman picked up the ball and threw it beyond the courtyard.

With the allure of the ripples forgotten, Ferret sped after the ball, barking excitedly as he went.

"He's my most fervid companion," he laughed. "Good boy!" He patted Ferret on the head as he took the retrieved ball from his jaws. "We'll play again soon. But now we must eat."

Lunch was enjoyed in the warmth of the kitchen, with Mr and Mrs March joining Roman at the table.

Hours idled away, consumed with resonating talks of Roman's life beyond that of Lyon House.

Mrs March had listened with a keen interest in his education and travels, herself having never left the village, so found that she was living precariously through his vivid memories of life. But throughout all the years he regaled away, there was never a single mention of the prospect of a future *Mrs* Lyons.

So, when Mr March excused himself to tend to his duties, she tactfully asked Roman, "may I speak freely, sir?"

"Why, of course. You have my ear, always." He leaned forward in his chair, expectantly.

"Are we to expect the arrival of a Mrs Lyons?"

Roman laughed. "Mrs March! Wherever did that notion come from?"

"Forgive me, sir," she said with a polite smile. "It's only that – well – you're such a striking man. I must admit, I'm quite surprised you've not taken a wife.

"I've never lacked for women vying for my affection, I assure you," he laughed. "Indeed, I've had more than my fair share," he added, settling back into his chair with easy comfort. "I've traveled the world, and I can say with absolute certainty – the love I seek does not exist."

His gaze fell into the depths of the fire, the flickering flames reflected in his eyes. "Not in this lifetime, anyway."

"Don't say that, sir," came the quiet reply.

"I fear it to be true... From the moment of inception, the soul embarks on a journey, searching. And when we're born, we live a life threaded with happiness, sadness, hope, and despair – the natural cycle of existence. Yet, most of us depart this world never having grasped its meaning.

The journey is endless, and for those who truly understand the path fate has laid before them, it's tireless. I know the meaning of *my* life, Mrs March, and count myself among the rare and fortunate few who possess such knowledge.

It is to nourish the body and seek one's soulmate – to become whole. That, in my view, is the true meaning of life. Yet loneliness remains the forever loyal companion of those who understand too much. And I pay that price willingly."

"The love you seek might be closer than you think."

"What do you mean?"

"Well, sir, you've traveled the world, met dignitaries, royalty, and a great many women, it seems. Yet the love you so desperately yearn for – perhaps it's been near all along."

A mischievous look embraced his eyes as he replied. "My dear Mrs March, you forget yourself. May I remind you – you're a married woman," he smiled. "Mr March would surely have my hide if I dared steal you away."

"I'm sure there's some days he'd love to *give* me away!" she laughed heartily.

"How I've missed your humour," he chuckled.

"And how I'm sure I'll come to appreciate *yours*, Master Roman," she guffawed.

"I'm very light of heart. Yet heavy of soul – for everywhere I go, the house and its reputation precedes me tenfold. I've yet to meet someone who hasn't begun a conversation with tales of Lyon House and its many misgivings over the years.

So, you see, even if I didn't know whom I sought, what woman in her right mind would willingly tether herself to the Master of Lyon House?"

"Plenty, I'm sure!" came the emphatic reply. "Have you not looked in the mirror? You're a true vision to behold – winsome inside and out."

Abashed, he looked away from her stare, blushing profusely.

"I speak the truth, Master Roman – your value is immeasurable. Not in wealth or status, but in the depth of your character, the kindness of your heart, and the strength of your spirit."

"You're too kind – you humble me." He held her gaze, his smile soft and fleeting. "I'm well aware of my 'value' – every room I enter is filled with whispers and scrutiny. But I care nothing for wealth, fame, or lineage. Society's laws and expectations mean little to me, and class divides even less. To me, a woman's true beauty radiates from within, and I've yet to find it. When I marry, Mrs March, it will be for the deepest of loves – a soulmate's love. You see now how rare and precious the love I seek truly is. The Lyons line will end before I wed for anything less. Nothing surpasses one's soulmate. Wouldn't you agree?"

"I do, sir. I do indeed. I believe my Mr March to be one such love."

"Then I'm honoured to be in your presence. To your prestige of such completeness, I can only dare but dream." He stood from his chair and bowed respectfully. "I've taken up far too much of your time. I'll take my leave of you and won't keep you any longer. Besides, I'm sure you must be quite weary of me by now."

"Not at all, sir."

"My dear Mrs March, once again, you are too kind... Might I lunch with you daily? Here, in the kitchen?" He laughed. "I promise I won't keep you shackled to my presence this long at every meal – but I have truly enjoyed your company."

"Why, of course! Mr March and I would be delighted."

"Very good... No doubt I'll see you here and there about my travels, for I must explore the house, see how the old girl has changed."

He chose to avoid the basement and second floor, not wishing his sudden presence to unsettle Mrs March or Miss Leighton – lest they assume he was inspecting the house for any impropriety. In contrast, his movements across the ground and first floors would seem far more natural, allowing for chance encounters, as these spaces were occupied by the family.

He stood in the dining room beside the window looking out for what should have been a perfectly manicured lawn and distant glints of the ocean. But impeding his view was the dense bulk of fog.

In London, they called it 'a real peasouper'. He would bet them all his money in the world if they did not agree that this fog before him now looking fixedly back at him from beyond the window, was indeed *worse* than the most dreadful of the peasoupers any Londoners had ever seen.

It was unearthly how it remained undaunted. It was as though the house had been lifted, then plunged within an ashen firepit. It was genuinely phenomenal, a remarkable sight in all its strangeness, for he did not mind the fog, not one slightest.

However, he *was* looking forward to the sea view and air that came with Lyon House. His travels abroad had conceded him inland, so he hoped the fog would soon lift so he could take a turn about the grounds with Ferret.

As a child, he spent many troubled times in the dining room. He was extremely picky with food choices, but of course, he was told by his father to eat everything on his plate that was served up for him.

He remembered one meal that consisted of overly fatty meat, potatoes, and a serving of vegetables that contained carrots. He was happy to consume the potatoes and vegetables, but all else turned his sensitive little stomach into knots.

His refusal to eat enraged his father, resulting in the punishment of remaining at the table until every bite had been consumed. Oh, how he had wept.

For hours he sat miserably, watching his parents outside on the lawn blithely playing croquet in the silken summer sun. With now and again, his mother's anguished face looking toward the dining room, his father dismissing her concerns.

His father assigned Mrs March to ensure all food was eaten. At that time, she was a housemaid, not the housekeeper. She had been instructed to inspect his plate every fifteen minutes.

Three hours had gone painfully by, when in due course, she had returned for her inspection.

The detestable food still lay dormant, cold, and congealed on his plate, but she had dismissed him and removed the plate from the table.

Later that day, he overheard a conversation, or rather, report, between Mrs March and his father concerning the luncheon, in which she had replied, 'everything, sir. He ate everything like the good little boy he is.'

Oh, how he longed to run to her and hold her tight. That day, she became his savior – his heroine. He knew, without a doubt, that whatever he confided in her would remain forever unspoken.

Good old Mrs March – what a kind soul she was.

As he meandered through the house, he found it strangely larger than he remembered. Perhaps it was the furnishings? His parents had filled the space with the finest ornamentations money could buy. Large, imposing family portraits adorned the walls, alongside fashionable depictions of various interests.

But none, he noticed, were of him. Nor could he find a single photograph. He had sent countless pictures of himself over the years, enclosed within letters exchanged with his mother. And yet, now that he was here, their whereabouts remained unseen.

Upstairs was the same – plenty of family portraits, yet none of him. Nothing. He searched every bedroom, even his parents', but not a single trace of his existence remained.

He rifled through cupboards, drawers, and wardrobes still filled with his parents' belongings, but among them – nothing. Not even the self-portraits he had sketched on the finest parchment, chronicling his ageing.

His mother had once written back in excitement, praising his talent and exclaiming how clever – how handsome – he was.

He had reached the conclusion that his parents believed in superstitions and talks of curses encircling Lyon House. How silly of them to not have an image of their only child anywhere in the house due to such irrational thoughts and notions.

It was common wisdom among the elders of today that photographs could capture an unsuspecting soul. But did they believe one's essence was likewise imprisoned within a portrait? Or even a simple pencil drawing?

What silly nonsense!

He would break this childish superstition and begin a self-portrait.

The fog had made it clear to him that he must stay within the limits of the house. So, he must do something to amuse himself, and that, he surmised, would be it.

He had already found the perfect place for the mural and would commence painting it tomorrow, right at the foot of the staircase in the staircase hall. One could not miss it there; it was the largest area of paintable wall in the house.

The things he would need to begin the project were already amongst his belongings in his bedroom, which was the furthest away from his parents' room. In fact, the opposite end of the house, giving way to the distasteful theme of 'children should be seldom seen, and of course, almost indefinitely, very rarely heard.' That task fell to the nanny, though of her he could not remember much, only that she was as kind as they came.

Tomorrow, he would leave his mark on Lyon House – make it feel his presence, remind it that he had returned.

Whether the house welcomed him or not was of little consequence.

It would know he was here.

Chapter 16

Roman's first night in the house passed in restful sleep. Thank Heavens he'd had the foresight to inform Mrs March that he took no breakfast and did not wish to be disturbed in the mornings – otherwise, he might have found her somewhat perplexed. For had woken at half past eleven.

He lay motionless, enveloped in the clement, soothing embrace of his bed sheets, listening – just as he had as a child – for the sounds of wildlife. But there was nothing. Not a single distant call or rustling leaf, only a dull, heavy silence that confirmed the fog still loitered.

Just as well, he had weeks of painting ahead of him.

After lunch with the March's, he would set up all his necessary tools, brushes, and paints, then begin. He felt enlivened about it, for he loved the solitude of his own company.

For days he worked religiously on his mural, only stopping for dinner, and sometimes working late into the night. All the while, Ferret lay conscientiously on the floor watching his Master work.

Mrs March came and went with trays of afternoon tea, though often they sat untouched – forgotten in the depths of his concentration. He was vaguely aware of Miss Leighton flickering about, busy with her tasks, yet the world beyond his easel seemed distant, unreal.

The only reality was himself and the painting – such was his immersion.

"Roman..." the strange voice slowly whispered.

"Hmm?" he replied dreamily, still focused on his work.

"Roman..."

"Yes, Mrs March, what is it?"

"Roman..."

"Mrs March, you do indeed have my attention," he answered abruptly as he turned around having been ripped from out of his almost meditative state. "What is it, my dear lady?" Upon seeing no sign of Mrs March, he called out for her. "Mrs March?" When no reply was forthcoming, he called out again, his temper waning. "Mrs March?!"

He placed his easel and brush on the adjacent table, which held spare paints, cloths, and a pot of water, and proceeded to look for her.

He investigated the grand hall; she was not there. So, he ventured into the corridor that led to the dining room at one end, and the orangery and conservatory at the other.

But still, there was no sign of her.

Perhaps his heightened concentration had made him hear things? Mrs March was not the sort of woman to call upon the Master of the house without cause.

So, he dismissed it as a temporary derangement of the mind – the kind only an artist experiences when truly drowning in the depths of their work.

He sighed, returning to his painting, picking up his easel and brush. As he leaned in to complete the nearly finished face, he heard his name again – called in a hushed, longing tone, distant and impossible to place.

Exasperation crept over him, his head growing hot, the first throbs of a headache beginning to take hold.

"Mrs March?!" he called out angrily. "Mrs Ma..."

His shout faltered – cut off by a long, drawn-out murmur, barely more than a breath. It stretched through the silence, wavering, elusive. And yet, it came from directly in front of him.

"Roman..."

He stared at the artwork, stricken, his breath unsteady as confusion gripped him. The situation was absurd, impossible – and yet, something deep within him refused to dismiss it.

His heart whispered that the voice came from the hidden recesses of the painting itself, but his mind battled against the notion, rejecting it as pure folly.

Then –

"Roman," it breathed.

Stronger now, unmistakable. The voice did not merely linger in the air. It seeped from the mural itself, crawling into his ears like an undeniable truth.

He could no longer pretend otherwise.

It was coming from the painting.

He leaned in closer still, studying the self-portrait's eyes – vague, distant, yet undeniably fixed upon him.

"Roman!" the voice rang out, sudden and sharp.

He jolted back, his head snapping away from the painting as though struck – an unseen force shoving him backward. Stumbling sideways, his hip caught the edge of the table, sending his paints and water crashing to the floor in a clatter that shattered the silence.

Mrs March appeared. "Whatever's the matter, sir?" she asked, shocked and breathless. "You're as white as that stallion you're painting."

"Roman…" the voice murmured – thin, fading, unraveling into the still air.

"Sir? Are you all right?"

He stood there, motionless, staring at Mrs March, uncertainty clouding his expression. A shadow of questioning lingered in his eyes, yet his lips did not form the words.

"Roman…" echoed the painting.

Then reasoning dawned on him – she could not hear the voice – only him.

His hand weakened, and the easel slipped from his grasp, sending forth a smattering of splintered hues across the dark wooden floor.

"Sir, you've been working too hard on this mural. You need to rest awhile – and eat." She gently grasped his elbow and guided him silently into the drawing room.

Inside, an untamed, roaring fire blazed, eager to envelop in warmth whoever chose to sit beside it.

She guided him into one of the chairs closest to its glow. "Stay there, if you will," she said gently. "I'll return shortly with a nice cup of hot chocolate."

"Thank you, Mrs March," he replied both grimly yet thankfully.

As he sat patiently awaiting her return, he mulled over his thoughts. It had undeniably been a woman's voice calling his name – clear, distinct. And yet, Ferret had never reacted to it, not even once.

That fact alone led him to a single, logical conclusion: the voice belonged to his imagination. It was not that he alone had heard something real. No, this voice had come from within – the recesses of his very own mind.

Perhaps Mrs March was right? Perhaps I *have* been working too hard on the mural. Engaging in a craft can be exhausting.

As promised, Mrs March duly returned, boasting a large cup of hot chocolate and a small selection of light snacks – a few neatly arranged biscuits, some buttered slices of toast, and a handful of sugared almonds.

"There you go, sir. Be careful though; it's very hot," she cautioned, setting the tray before him with practiced care.

"Thank you Mrs March." He reached out for the cup and placed it down immediately onto the side table. "You told no lies," he smiled. "It's *very* hot... May I ask where you were earlier?"

"Why, of course. I'd been into the village to pick up a few things. I like to personally choose the meat, fruit, and vegetables before having them delivered – it ensures we get the best quality.

I'd just returned when I heard that almighty crash – the table, your paints, everything tumbling to the floor. Was it Ferret?"

He glanced at Ferret, the loyal creature nestled at his side. Stroking his head with quiet affection, he sighed. "I confess, it was me." His smile was weak, almost sheepish. "I got carried away with painting, and before I knew it, the whole lot had met the floor. My apologies if I caused any alarm."

"Not at all, sir."

"And Miss Leighton," he pressed. "Where was she?"

"Oh, Miss Leighton has been in the kitchen wing, baking. It's her afternoon off today, but she likes to bake in her spare time – which I allow of course. If the baked goods were not of my exacting standards, and delicious as they are, she would not be permitted to do so, I can assure you of that. The cakes you enjoy with your afternoon teas are baked, care of Miss Leighton. You do approve, do you not?"

"Why of course I do, thank you. You may inform Miss Leighton how satisfying her baked goods are."

"I will." she smiled. "She'll be pleased to hear it. Will there be anything else, sir? I must begin preparations for dinner."

"Not for me, thank you. Just a light spread on a tray served in my bedroom. I think I'll retire for the evening."

"Are you quite sure there's nothing else you need?"

"Quite sure. I'll remain here and finish my hot chocolate; then, I'll go up. Goodnight, Mrs March."

"Goodnight to you, sir. I'll send Mr March up later with a tray."

"That will do nicely. Thank you."

For the next hour, he sat gazing into the fire, cradling the now-lukewarm hot chocolate in both hands, sipping absentmindedly.

With quiet preoccupation, he watched as shifting shapes and fleeting scenes emerged within the embers, flickering through the mouldings of the coals.

How utterly raw and true a fire was – yet how deceptive, how deadly.

Having drained the last of his drink, he placed the empty cup back onto its saucer and stood, stretching from the chair. "Come along, Ferret. Let's go to bed," he said arduously.

Ferret, in turn, stood up and stretched in conformity with his Master.

"There's a good boy."

Ferret led the way out of the drawing room and through into the staircase hall.

Roman noticed the mess had been cleared and cleaned away. There was no urge to return to his painting; he passed it without a glance.

As he ascended the stairs, a coldness pressed in – not of winter, but of something else. It encased him like crushed ice, creeping into his breath, his bones.

Then, the sound came – drawn-out, suppressed, almost swallowed by the silence – the voice drifted from the mural, stretched thin and spectral, hollow and distant, like breath caught between the living and the dead.

"Goodnight, Roman..."

Chapter 17

After finishing the light meal from the platter that Mrs March had sent up, Roman placed the tray outside his door and went to bed.

He had fitful dreams that night.

He dreamed he was aboard the Titanic in the final moments of its sinking. But he was not as he was now – he was a child, just ten years old, the same age he had been when he was sent away from Lyon House.

He dreamt he was sliding down the deck of the ship toward the hungry, white frothing water that quickly bellowed up near him.

He could feel his mother holding his hand tightly, and when their warm bodies met the cold, deep water – it stung.

Oh, how it stung, the pain was gruesome.

His mother shouted something – words lost, swallowed at first by the strident rasp of the vicious water.

The ship bowed, cracked, and split – booming, groaning as it relinquished itself to the ocean.

Then she said it again. "Hold your breath, my darling!"

And as the water embraced his chin, he instinctively breathed in one last gasp of air; then they spiralled down into the dragging depths of the sea.

He held his breath with valiant resolve as they plunged deeper – ever darker – into the ungodly, ice-cold abyss. It was so bitterly frigid that it seared through him, a fire born of the depths.

It devoured his ears and nose first, merciless in its hunger. Then, as if an afterthought, daggers of ice stabbed into his eyes.

Panic seized him. He thrashed against the weight of the water, but it bore down – unyielding, unrelenting.

How malicious and cruel it felt.

His mother's grip tightened.

How she loved him so.

He wanted to scream so fiercely. How he *longed* to scream; but was muzzled with the waters repressing might.

How he longed to breathe.

His lungs felt as though they were filling with frozen nettles – how they prickled so.

How he wanted to go home.

How he longed to breathe.

Feeling as though he would shatter, he took that longed for, sweet nectarous breath.

Water surged down his throat, ferocious and merciless, like icicles slicing through flesh. His ears popped – then, silence.

All but a single, high-pitched drone of endless isolation.

He felt as if he had cracked open.

He felt so much pain that had lightning effectuated upon him to lift him from his misery; he would not have felt a thing.

He inhaled more water until his poor body could take no more.

His mother's grip loosened as he became heavy, yet light and calm. How strangely calm he felt.

Then, he was still. Still, and watching.

He watched blankly as he sensed his mother's hand brush unmoving across his cheek before sinking down and away from him.

How he loved his mother so.

An eternity seemed to pass as he longed to die.

Then nothing remained but total darkness, silence, hopelessness, and release.

He woke from his dream clutching his throat, sobbing sorrowfully. The air was so thick and still he could barely breathe, like some remnant of the dream still stirred.

But now, in reality, it was *warm* salty water that flooded and drenched his skin – a reality that secretly crippled him with grief that tore at his heart and ravaged his soul.

He remained motionless for a period, enveloped in his sorrow, reflecting on his parents and the revelations brought forth by the dream.

Then he felt the pull of remorse towards his parents' room.

He walked in darkness along the corridor, his only guiding light being that of the window at the end – the fog had allowed a breath of moonlight to numb the warmth and vibrancy from out of the stained glass, only permitting smears of cold whites and cool blues to seep through and melt upon the floor in a brittle transparent layer.

When he reached his parents' bedroom, he opened the door without hesitation. But the moment he stepped inside, something shifted. The air pressed against him – stifling, thick – filling him with a hesitation that had not been there before.

The room did not feel entirely real.

His vision wavered, distorting the space around him. It was as if two identical photographs had been layered atop one another, but misaligned – subtly fractured, slightly wrong.

Not straying far from the security of the doors frame, he looked into the jet-black obscureness that lay out unwelcomely before him. His only shaft of light being that of the window behind him, which brought forth a weak manifestation of his shadow that embellished the patch of elongated dingy light underfoot.

From the bed, a dim, unearthly glow seeped into the darkness. He dared not turn on the light – afraid it might be swallowed whole. So, with cautious steps, he edged toward it, trepidation coiling in his chest.

What he saw defied all laws and rules of scientific understanding, and nature – the spectre, of which he chose to refer it, lay as if soundly asleep. But not *on* the bed. Nor floating above it as one would expect such a damnation.

No, this creature, this being – whatever it was, was laid half-submerged within the very fathoms of the bed itself.

Its sustenance moved in a slight way, like wispy white clouds forming a known solid shape for the human brain to recognise and therefore comprehend. And to *his* brain, the convergence of matter looked as though it were that of a woman. Although there were no facial features, one could see the definite hulk of breasts heaving as it breathed.

He wanted to call for someone – anyone, so they could observe and confirm what he was seeing. So, he would know that he was not going mad.

But no matter how hard he tried, he could not find his voice – he remained silent, and he remained transfixed.

He dared to reach out and lay a hand upon its wavering mass. It felt more solid than appeared, with the texture giving the pretence of cold mist.

He leaned in closer, intently watching its incarnating face, patiently awaiting the proclamation of identity.

But almost as if the spectre knew of his expectations, it slowly dissolved, immersing itself away back into the nothingness whence it came, leaving him once again within a deluge of darkness.

He ran to the light switch and snapped it on, the sudden blast of bright light giving way to momentary blindness.

But once his eyes had refocused on the bed, he could see it.

There was no denying it – proof, undeniable, that something had been there.

On the bed lay a perfect indentation – a concavity, unmistakable, shaped like a humanoid figure.

And suddenly finding his voice, he shouted out, "Mrs March!!"

Chapter 18

Ferret lay beside the fire in the bathroom twitching erratically and barking mildly at something in his dreams. The fire, as if in eagerness to wake him, crackled resoundingly with each interlocking twist and turn of its lucent lustrous yellow flames. They thrust themselves up the chimney as if in effort for their sharp tips to dazzle above the very stack itself. As it vigorously flicked and flashed, it highlighted perfectly the otherwise dark regions of the bathroom.

Roman lay, eyes closed, relaxing in the bath, encased and comforted in a deeply filled hot smother of water. His mood was sombre as his thoughts about last night preyed heavily on his mind.

He was musing about the spectre, and how strange it had felt beneath the weight of his hand.

One would usually expect one's hand to pass through such a thing as *it* was indeed doing to the bed. But when he touched it, it was as though it were pushing back, like it was trying to solidify.

His hand remained cold for hours after, the chill clinging stubbornly to his skin. To his dismay, tiny droplets of condensation had begun to gather upon it – proof of something unnatural.

When he returned to the bed for further investigation, the imprint was gone. Vanished. As though it had never been there at all.

He was profoundly grateful that Mrs March had not heard his call. Had she come to his aid, she would have found nothing amiss and, at the very least, deemed him irrational.

She had stood before him, unshaken, as the voice from the mural wove its murmurs – again and again. Yet she had heard not a single one of its mystifying whispers. Indeed, her face had looked at *him* with alarm.

He was quite sure that Ferret also looked at him with an air of unease.

If his father were here, he would tell him that it was unhealthy to take seriously what is just a morbid misdirection and insensibility of the mind. That it was merely a dalliance with frivolousness. That it was all nonsense and to cease stoking the flames of ridiculousness, and to ignore it.

His mother though, if *she* were here, she would believe him conclusively. She would help him make sense of and seek out rationality and explanations through intense investigations, before finally dismissing it to be nothing *other* than otherworldly.

He rose slightly from the bath, realisation widening his eyes. If she – his esteemed mother – had believed in the possible curse of Lyon House, then did that not make it real?

Through this very line of thinking, a vague understanding surfaced. It was she, not his father, who had insisted he be sent away as a boy. She had done it to protect him – because she loved him deeply.

He still remembered it vividly. That night. The moment he was plucked from his home. The moment he was torn from the love and warmth of his mother's embrace.

He had managed to snatch away the brooch she wore at her neck, clutching it tightly for months after. It brought him a quiet, fragile comfort – until the last traces of her perfume finally faded.

It bore the shape of a diamond, its bright white, old mine-cut diamonds arranged in precise, open scrollwork of darkened silver. Flawlessly symmetrical, each side mirrored the other without fault.

At its heart lay a large emerald, its pear-shaped counterpart dangling regally below. Both gems shimmered with a vibrant blue-green hue, a striking contrast that brought out her eyes exceedingly well.

His mother's eyes were engaging shades of verdigris, so wearing the brooch offset her eyes and piece quite handsomely. It had been a gift to her from his father to memorialise their first wedding anniversary. She had worn it always and had each of her outfits matched around it.

She wore no other jewellery except for that. She said there was no need for anything more, that she would never *want* for anything more.

He still had the brooch, keeping it safe among his most personal and treasured possessions. It would remain there until the day fate decreed he meet the woman he would one day be fortunate enough to proudly call his wife.

Then, it would belong to her.

It is what his mother would wish for.

It is what *he* wished.

It was now clear to him that his mother did indeed believe there to be a curse attached to Lyon House. For why else would she have sent him away? Her only child. He, the son, and heir to the Lyon House estate, never to be seen again.

He understood now why there were no images of him anywhere in the house – no trace, no reflection of his existence. He had come to believe that his mother had hoped the house would overlook him entirely, banishing him from its thoughts as though he had never belonged.

His notions now slowly resigning, he slipped deeper and sleepily into the cradle of water, where he stay motionless for several moments. He felt comforted within the state of limbo in which the water grasped him.

He enjoyed the feeling of freedom and solace until the indistinct stirrings of song broke through and seized him.

The sound that drifted towards him was one of nature at its most impeccable.

It was the most enrapturing thing he had ever heard.

He dared not move, fearing that even the slightest disturbance would ripple through the water, shattering the symphonious, beguiling song – an enchantment his ears were fortunate enough to hear.

It was celestial.

It was chilling.

His heart began to beat heavily as he felt compelled to go in search of it.

He rose steadily and noiselessly from the bath, reaching down for his trousers that lay beside the unperturbed Ferret. He eased into them steadily, the material beginning to thirstily drink away the excess water that ran down his legs.

He followed the ribbons of melody along the corridor – the vibration of which was so strong, he felt sure he could see it.

The ribbons were forming plaits, the plaits laced through the membrane of the house with such a force, he felt like he was saturated in the sirenic profoundness of an intricate ethereality.

He shuffled down the corridor, his gait slow, his body stiffened. His mind raced – swift, alert. Yet it conjured the illusion of exaggerated lethargy.

As he passed the staircase, he was dimly aware of Mrs March standing in a fit of dismay. She was looking beyond him; in the direction he had come from. Her mouth moved sluggishly and soundlessly. He could not make sense of it.

He did not *want* to make sense of it.

His only care was that of the alluring, magnetic cords that pulled him nearer to the enthralling sound that took prisoner of his entire consciousness.

The closer he got, the more overpowering it became.

The lure was irrepressible.

He closed his eyes, tears forming. When he opened them, he found himself standing outside his parents' bathroom, the door of which was slightly ajar.

Zeal overtook him, the urgency to unearth the voice's owner driving him forward.

He seized the door, opening it fiercely.

It slammed into the wall aggressively with a ferocious bang.

He stood now at the centre of the coil of sound, its vibrant echoes reduced to a hum – soft, melodic, like a bird's sweetest song.

Then, as though the spell were broken, all became silent, and all became still.

He gazed searchingly into the empty bathroom, quickly becoming dispirited and cold, and was relieved to feel the warmth of a blanket shrouding his shoulders – he was unaware that he was half-naked and wet.

He was unaware of Mrs March reprimanding the hapless Miss Leighton.

He was unaware he entered the corridor the same moment Miss Leighton had exited the linen store carrying a pile of neatly folded laundry. The shock of seeing him had caused her to drop everything she held to the floor.

He could now hear the voice of Mrs March breaking through the fortification of peculiar silence that held him firmly within its grip.

As he made to answer her, he began to shake uncontrollably, be it with cold, be it with shock, be it with fear, or be it with all – he did not know.

"Nothing to concern yourself with, Mrs March," he said sedately. "Everything's all right."

"Very well, sir," she replied, concern in her voice.

As he made his way down the corridor towards his bedroom, a final verse of the melancholic melody taunted him lethargically in subdued tones.

When at last he reached the sanctum of his room, he closed the door with an arduous sigh, as silence once again enveloped him.

Chapter 19

Roman sat quietly in the darkened drawing room beside the fire. He stared moodily into its roaring belly, willing it to burn away his self-doubts and torturous thoughts. The clock had barely struck six and was already as dark as night.

He looked at Ferret, who was stretched out on a rug in front of it. How he longed for the innocent mind that only an animal could possess.

He lifted the large, full glass of brandy he held up to his lips and took from it a long, deep, full-bodied sip. It felt luxurious as its warmth gently caressed his throat and slipped down to his eagerly awaiting stomach. This was his second glass now, so he was feeling the mild effects of inebriation.

He settled himself more deeply into the accommodation of the chairs seat and looked at the fire once again, sighing deeply. "Perhaps I should never have returned, Ferret," he spoke out grimly.

Ferret looked to his Master and gave him an almost look of understanding before exuding a slight yelp as he settled back down to enjoy his basking in the resplendence of the fire.

"For now I am back, I feel the house's gaze fixed firmly upon me like it's watching, waiting, and biding its time. I feel as though I am a fish, the house the bowl, and its soul, or lifeforce shall we say – the cat. It plays and toys with me to no end." He took several hearty gulps of the brandy. "Perhaps beginning the self-portrait was a mistake. For now, I fear the house has taken my soul – firmly embedded, entwined with its own. It began the moment my brush touched the wall, and with each passing day, it deepens. Do you like living here, Ferret? At Lyon House?"

Ferret pricked his ears with attention at the mention of his name.

Roman reached down to Ferret and stroked him, continuing his one-sided conversation.

"I'm of sound mind, Ferret – you know that as well as anyone. Yet even I cannot fathom the sights that meet my eyes or the sounds that bore into my ears.

I have always believed there's a practical explanation for everything.

But now; now I believe the sanity I once held so dear is being drained away by a wraith of some sort. I'm haunted both day and night by something which I cannot explain.

I am tormented. Even in my dreams.

The most desolate of things have been occurring to me, Ferret. And now, all I see before me is a long, lonely, bleak, and unstable path that leads directly to my unjust."

He emptied the smooth, delectable liquid into his mouth and swallowed as if it contained every last vestige of hope he had.

"What do you have to say about it, hmm? Are there really such things as ghosts and curses? Or am I simply yielding to the hysterics of others? Perhaps I have follies within a childish mind. After all, I do find myself speaking aloud to uncomprehending ears that might not care even if they did understand." He smiled halfheartedly as he reached for the bottle of brandy that sat upon the table beside him.

A knock at the door refrained him.

"Come," he answered.

The door opened to admit Mrs March, who carried with her an expression of concern.

"My dear Mrs March. What on earth ails you?" He stood and beckoned for her to be seated in the vacant chair which sat at the other side of the fireplace. "Would you care to join me?" he asked, whilst gesturing toward an unused glass beside the bottle.

"Thank you, sir, but no," she replied as she sat primly into the chair.

"As you wish," he responded, whilst re-taking his seat.

"I thought I heard voices, sir?" she asked, while looking about the room.

"Voices?"

"Yes, sir. I thought you had company, so wanted to inquire if there'd be an extra place setting needed for dinner."

"No, Mrs March. My only company is Ferret here – I'm divulging to him my innermost thoughts and feelings, brought on by this." He reached for the bottle of brandy and refilled his glass. "Though if I were to enlighten him with the secrets of The Universe, it would mean no more to him than the simple pleasure the heat and glow of that fire brings," he finished with a burdensome smile.

"Are you all right, sir?" she asked with concern as she watched him consume numerous drinks from his glass.

"My dear Mrs March, if I were to tell you my afflictions, you would no doubt leave me and Lyon House. Both you *and* Mr March. Just as Miss Leighton has done. I heard your hushed tones from the library the other day. Whispers are really quite loud when all else is silent."

"I must insist you don't burden yourself with the reasons of Miss Leighton's departure from Lyon House. Her circumstances are quite her own to bear."

"No doubt, from her lips, stories of horror and dread will emerge – fueling a renewed wave of gossip, all in the name of the supposed curse of Lyon House."

He looked at her with avid interest as he awaited her reply.

"You must pay no mind to idle tongues wagging without restraint. What Lyon House has endured is nothing more than a series of unfortunate events. These gossipmongers revel in wild misconceptions, spreading them like wildfire. Their tongues ought to be stilled." She shook her head in disgust.

"So, you don't believe in curses then?"

"Of course not. They're simply a figment of one's imagination."

"So, you would believe by denying their existence, renders them powerless and untrue?"

"Yes. Accepting their existence fuels them and therefore makes them true."

The vehement inverse of her answer to his question silenced him momentarily. "So, if you starve it, it will perish. And if you feed it, it will thrive."

"Yes, sir," she answered with a smile.

The next drink he took was one of courage. "And what of ghosts, Mrs March?" he asked with a roguish smile in the hope that it masked the seriousness of his question. "What's your opinion of those?"

"I don't believe in such things."

"Do you not think that we're more than mortal flesh? That we hold within us a spirit and soul? That when we're stripped of this body, our ghost, or replica shall we say, remains?"

"Of a soul, yes, of that I agree. But as for ghosts and replicas of oneself, I suspect we see what we want to see and believe what we want to believe. The mind is a mighty thing – if we allow it, it will conspire against us, confuse, and misinform, reducing us to a flurry of misinterpretation."

He pondered on her words for a while whilst looking into his glass. He circulated the dark liquor around, enjoying the tiny vortex he created.

"But how does one discern fact from misinterpretation and fiction?"

"Well, sir, if others experience our misinterpretation, then it, of course, must be fact. But if others don't share and experience our 'facts', then it is non-other than fiction."

"And if the two become one, and hopelessness sets in and blackens the mind?"

"We must have patience with the facts, sir. Only then can we reveal the masquerades of the detestable fiction and misinterpretations… We all have dark times. Mr March is fond of saying – 'only the most beautiful and perfect of things can grow and nurture from out of the soil that is enriched with dark…'" She cleared her throat and lowered her voice slightly before continuing. "Pardon me, sir – 'shit.'" she finished with a blush.

Upon receiving this information, he laughed heartily. It had been a considerable period since he had experienced such genuine amusement. Speaking with Mrs March had lightened his burden tenfold.

"Why, Mrs March! Had I not been calmed by my enjoyment of this exceptional brandy, I would've been quite surprised to hear your detailed account of Mr March's saying."

"He says it how it is, sir. As do I."

"And I thank you *both* for it."

"I believe everything happens for a reason, sir. I have faith it's always for the greater good. Now, sir, if you don't mind, I must take my leave of you. I have dinner to prepare."

"Forgive me. Time has run away from us, has it not." He smiled as they both rose from their chairs.

She walked towards the door, and as she opened it to leave, said, "'tis better to light one candle than to curse the darkness, sir."

"I sincerely apologise for any moments of hysteria or delirium I may have subjected you to. It was never my intention to burden you with such displays."

"The grieving process is unsurmountable. One needs no apologies for that. Good evening to you, sir."

"Good evening, Mrs March. And thank you, your words have lightened thoughts that were previously full of lead."

They exchanged smiles before she closed the door.

As she walked down the corridor and away from the drawing room, she was ashamed to admit that she had heard every word he had given away to Ferret. For she had stood, quite disturbed, before the door listening worryingly to all he had said.

She had been induced towards the drawing room by the sound of conversation. So did truthfully wish to know if there were to be extra place settings for dinner – it was her duty to know.

She hesitated, uncertain whether to knock and enter, fearing he might mistake her for an eavesdropper. The doubt stalled her, leaving her unsure of what to do.

So, she lingered, silently praying for a moment of quiet before finally gathering the courage to knock.

She loved Master Roman dearly – he was like the child Mr March and she had never been able to have. More than anything, she hoped their conversation had eased his worries, bringing him some comfort. For it had only been six months now since the passing of his parents.

Grief could play all kinds of tricks to one's mind, and she would refuse to allow him to think that what he was going through was anything other than the mind processing his grief.

So, because of that, she was *glad* she had prevailed before the door. Had she not done so, he would never have unburdened his mind to her – if only partially so.

∞ ∞ ∞

Roman had continued to stand after the departure of Mrs March. His thoughts hanging on her every word.

Was grief to be the scientific explanation of which he craved and needed?

He felt kindled to fate for sending her to him whilst his thoughts were so dire. For it was through her reckoning, he found a certain level of freedom and peace of mind.

He made his way over to the window and stared out into the evening's foggy drabness.

"This damned fog is relentless, Ferret. For weeks now it's draped over the house like a soddened white veil."

Ferret looked at his Master as though he understood, barking heartily before surrendering himself once more to the only words that mattered in this moment – those whispered by the fire, interlaced between its restless flames.

Roman pressed his hand against the window's cold glass, its temperature imbuing him with a sense of refreshment and crisp relief. The liquor had gone to his head, so he abandoned large gulps in favour of slow, intermittent sips – each one measured, deliberate. All the while, he searched for anything, anything at all, to stave off the creeping fog of blackness.

Something outside had unexpectedly caught his eye. A gash of movement that bled its way toward him.

Something of which, by the way it moved, was not of this physical world.

Whatever it was, it was moving closer toward the window.

Then, abruptly – only fractions away from the glass – a face.

A face of mist.

It lunged at the window with such force he was certain the pane would shatter, the apparition crashing upon him.

But just as swiftly as it had begun, the movement ceased – yet the face remained, silent, watching.

He stared at the soft features of the face as it held him in its mesmeric grip.

Time stood still, like he had been captured within the confines of a photograph to join the unanimated subjects inside.

Try as he may, he could not move.

His entire body was restrained and shackled by the very void that surrounded him.

The air he needed to breathe felt as if it were crushing every ounce of breath from out of his crumpling lungs.

And as the face hovered there, its only concern was that of his hand, which remained undeliberate and inert upon the shield of the windowpane, of which it analysed with intent scrutiny.

It was only when the glass of brandy escaped his other hand and dropped to the floor that the face recoiled back – receding as instantaneously as it had appeared, to settle within the prison of fog once again, from which it escaped.

It was then that he was released from its grip and able to stand back from the window, confounded.

Then, at last, he was able to speak – though only in a grave, barely audible tone.

"I have stared into the face of hopelessness and discontent...

I have lit that candle, Mrs March. For now, more than ever, I shall look toward its light.

Yet even as I say these words, the face – gaunt and spectral, still lingers in the darkness – a wraith of mist, shifting yet constant.

Watching.

Patient.

It waits beyond the flickering glow, knowing that all light must, eventually, extinguish."

Chapter 20

Mrs March prepared the evening dinner with great excitement. For once the meal was had and the table cleared, at ten o'clock sharp, she and Mr March were invited to spend the remainder of the evening with the Master in the drawing room.

He was to play for them, and how she looked forward to hearing him on the violin.

She had already set out Mr March's attire for the evening – he was to dress in his finest. As for herself, though always in the best her role as housekeeper allowed, she would change all the same and tidy her hair. The scent of cooking must not linger in the air while in the Master's company.

She had already resolved that tonight would be steeped in sadness. For the desire to hear the Master play was the very reason his parents had perished – never having had the chance, they had been on their way to New York aboard the Titanic.

She wiped away her tears as they drizzled finely down her cheeks. How proud his parents were of him and his many exceptional accomplishments. His mother was more so, for he was always his mother's son.

How her heart raced with the excitement of hearing such beauty she knew would exude from his performance this evening.

Sometimes, the Madame would read letters from Master Roman to her – oh, what accomplishments indeed!

He spoke several languages, was an exceptional artist, and had travelled the world, moving within circles so rarefied that even the 'who's who' of today were unaware of their existence – and never likely to be. Such was their wealth and eminence.

But his true forte was music, the violin his kindred spirit. He had no need for a score – for once he heard a piece, it was emblazoned upon his soul. He was, in every sense, one with the violin.

∞ ∞ ∞

Entering the drawing room and seeing the Master, Mrs March's heart swelled with pride. How handsome he looked – dressed in full formal wear, standing in quiet readiness beside the piano, awaiting Mr March and her arrival.

Resting upon the piano's dark, glossy surface, the violin and bow lay in patient anticipation of their Master's touch.

She glanced toward the chairs by the fire. He had moved them – they now faced away from the flames, turned instead toward the evening's true source of enthrallment: him.

How exuberant she felt, how deeply honoured. Yet sorrow lingered, a quiet ache in her chest. How she wished his parents could witness the man the boy had become. How the Madame, surely, would have wept with joy.

"Good evening, sir," the March's said in concordance.

"Mr and Mrs March!" He greeted them with a smile so radiant it could brighten even the darkest corners of the earth. "Good evening to you both. Please, make yourselves comfortable."

He gestured toward the waiting chairs he had carefully arranged. "Mrs March, before you take your seat, would you do me the honour of joining me at the piano for a leisurely warm-up? I haven't played a single note on the violin since my return to Lyon House three months ago, and I find myself positively electric with both excitement and trepidation. You would grant me the deepest gratitude if you were to accept my request."

Mrs March stood rigid with mortification as she replied. "But, sir," she spluttered out with a blush of discombobulation. "To your standards, I could only but dream!"

"Are you questioning my mother's opinion of you?"

"Sir?"

"In her letters, many times she would regale explicitly how exceptionally well you play. In particular, Beethoven's 'Moonlight Sonata' – her favourite piece. And, my dear Mrs March, that is no easy conquest. One must be a most proficient pianist to uphold such mastery. Upon my mother's word, I must insist you join me, for you are, so it would seem, as accomplished as I."

"But, sir, I don't hold a candle to you – nor to the fine musicians you perform with."

"Mrs March, it's not their flame I wish to see dance – it is yours. So, you see, your argument is quite futile."

He reached for her hand, bowing his head as his eyes met hers, steady and unwavering. "I refuse to accept anything less than a yes."

Conceding defeat, she placed her hand in his and allowed him to lead her and be comfortably seated before the piano.

"I've prepared the musical score for you – 'The Wedding Dance Waltz'. Do you know of it?"

"Oh, yes. It's a charming piece."

"Indeed, it is." He smiled, took his instruments, raised the violin to his neck, readied his bow, and said, "on my lead."

She maintained steady eye contact with him as she waited with trembling fingers and a nervously beating heart for the sound of his first few notes.

Then, with a slight, swift tilt of his head in acknowledgement of her joining him, she began to play.

He closed his eyes momentarily as the sweet, evocative music swept over him.

It felt enlivening to unite with his violin again. For he had not played a single note of it since the devastation of his parents passing. And though she did not know it, Mrs March joining him in his first triumphant chords was as much for his confidence as it was for her. She played wonderfully well, marrying his violin beautifully. His mother had recounted her talent remarkably well. He must ask her to play for him one evening, and quite soon.

When the final notes had been played out, he smiled at her with radiance. "How you must struggle so to keep such talent secret."

"I assure you, the secret keeps itself," she replied with a smile as she made her way over to be reseated with her husband. "It was a privilege to play with you, sir, thank you."

"Indeed, the privilege was all mine," he replied with a gracious bow of the head. "And now, it will be my highest of triumphs to play for you the arrangement of musical pieces of which I had appointed for my parents. The first of which – 'Granada'."

The March's watched as he played with such eloquence, splendour, and vigour. He was exceptional.

And although he played alone, Roman imagined the confounding sounds of the orchestra as the rest of the musicians joined him. Together, they were one sole instrument of fluent passion and artistry. They played 'Granada' with fervency, thrill, and delectation.

Before each piece was played, Roman cordially announced it: 'On the Beautiful Blue Danube'. 'Merry Widow Waltz'. 'Chambre Separee'. 'Tales of the Vienna Woods'. 'Wiener Blut'. 'Sphinx'. 'Lied Ohne Worte', and 'Emperor Waltz'.

"And for my final piece – 'Songe d'Automne'. I must confess this to being my best-loved piece. It never fails to enrapture me in its seduction."

The moment his bow lay upon the strings, he closed his eyes as if in transcendence.

Consuming feelings of intensity devoured him and encircled his soul with every note. He felt as though he had been lifted to another world.

He moved lightly and harmoniously about the room as if in dance with an unseen partner.

And when he transiently opened his eyes, the face at the window was fleeting but definite.

It was the same spectral face that once again hovered before the glazing. Only this time, it did not stare at him, but through him. It was as though he were not there – like *he* was the one out of time. Like *he* were the spectre, not *it*.

He turned his back to its empty stare, and closing his eyes once again, proceeded to sink his soul within the enigmatic grip of his music.

Had he opened his eyes, he would have seen the spectre embracing him as they danced.

And as the music came to its imminent and poignant diminuendo, with his final note having played out, he, at last, opened his eyes and the spectre that stood before him dropped as a stone would to the floor, and melted away beneath it.

He turned round quickly as the March's sudden standing ovation ruptured his still infatuated state.

"Bravo!... Bravo!" they shouted in harmony. "Oh, Master Roman sir! How proud your parents would've been!" enthused Mrs March whilst smudging away tears of exhilaration from her cheeks. "I've never heard such sublimity in all my days! How truly, truly astonishing you are, sir!"

"Be careful, Mrs March, or Mr March may need to widen the doors for my ego," he laughed.

"I wouldn't mind, sir," laughed Mr March.

"You're too generous." He laughed as he turned and placed his violin and bow down regardfully into its case, of which he had retrieved from underneath the piano. "This evening's been one of considerable indulgence. I thank you both most kindly for the pleasure of your company."

"Not at all, sir! Not at all!" Mrs March exclaimed. "The pleasure was indeed all ours to be had."

"Now, if you don't mind, I shall take my leave of you and retire for the evening."

"Certainly, sir. You must be very tired. Your performance tonight was truly remarkable and unforgettable," Mrs March responded.

Roman smiled and tipped his head obligingly at her words.

After good nights were exchanged, he called forth Ferret, and as Roman reached the door to leave, he turned and said to Mrs March, "I thank you deeply from the bottom of my heart for entertaining my mother on the evenings of which my father wasn't present."

"Of course, sir," she answered with a curtsey. "It was nothing. I enjoyed it just as much, if not more than she."

"Goodnight, Mrs March, Mr March."

"Goodnight, sir," they replied.

"And, Mrs March."

"Yes, sir?"

"I must insist you play for me. Soon."

"No honour could be greater."

The closing of the door established an end to his evening, and as he climbed the stairs wantingly for his bed, the sound of Ferret barking, mildly grated his nerves.

"What is it, Ferret?" he asked wearily, for he was in a state of slumber, such was his fatigue.

Ferret was sat, poised and observant beneath the uncompleted self-portrait of his Master. And although his tale was in a state of adventure, he was growling all but ever so slightly.

Roman steadied himself against the bannister and watched as Ferret seemed to interact with the painting.

And through the fit of barking, Roman could just make out the long, resonant voice exhaling through.

"Goodnight... Roman..."

Chapter 21

An excellent fire burned away in the library as Roman sat looking vacantly and unblinking into the vastness of its red and orange glow. Upon his lap, a book of Keats lay open and unread, the words on the pages no longer holding his interest. For now, he was intoxicated by his own words that rushed about his head in a dizzying whirr of complexing thoughts.

It was evident to him that Ferret, whom at this very moment lay demurely before the fire, was now indeed experiencing his fiction – which made it a fact.

He could no longer deny these plethoras of incidents as grief, fiction or dalliances in which he had succumbed – it was all too apparent to be fact, of which, had to be accompanied by an alternate explanation.

There was a reason for everything, and he would have to wait patiently for it to reveal itself to him.

In the meantime, he would abide by its rules and except its offerings when proffered – for it had been several uneventful days since the musical evening he had enjoyed with the March's.

He even had resumed working on his self-portrait, though being careful to avoid the peak times of its ghostlike whispers that plagued the painting every morning and evening – always as he passed by it.

And now he had grown so accustomed to it that if it were to cease, he would find some emptiness about him, for he no longer felt bewildered and dismayed. Acceptance, along with the evidence of Ferret now sharing his exposures had gratified him.

He sighed in serenity as he focused his gaze on the windows.

Since his return home, not a single seagull had called – no birdsong, no whisper of life. Everything lay in a state of encasement. The silence was so complete, it was deafening.

He longed for the hush of the sea, but the fog smothered all sound, sealing Lyon House in its grasp – deaf to the living world beyond.

By day, it cast the house in a pale, unnatural brightness; by night, an oppressive blackness, like a smudged chalkboard – its darkness dusting every corner, settling thick and unbroken.

He closed his eyes to rest, and when he opened them, it was late afternoon, and clinging to it was the final kindles of light.

Ferret was no longer sprawled statuesque before the fire, which had dimmed to a calm red glow. His gaze drifted lazily about the room in search of him, but instead of meeting Ferret's stare, his eyes caught something else – a strange reflection in the window.

It was the spectre.

It loomed beyond the glass, peering outward as it took shape before the window.

The human form within it was emerging, shifting, wavering. Now, it revealed itself in mortal colour – subtle, spectral, awash in pale opalescent hues. It hung in the air, motionless, yet flickering in and out like a failing electric lightbulb, struggling, straining, desperately mustering the strength to remain at full power.

He approached with careful, measured steps. And as though sensing his presence, the figure began to turn – slowly, languidly, as if submerged in the deepest of waters.

Its waist-length dark blonde hair drifted, repositioning in a dreamlike manner, revealing the first glimpse of a face – one most incomparable.

Upon it lay a veil of startlement, fragile and ghostly in its expression.

He experienced a sense of disorientation, realising that *he* had seemingly startled *it,* or as now became clear, *her.*

And as she sustained her deathly slow turn, their eyes cemented.

He reached out, his hand hovering before finally resting on her shoulder, gently drawing her nearer.

But in that instant, it was as though he had extinguished a light – she vanished abruptly, leaving him alone once more in the dimly lit room.

∞ ∞ ∞

Roman hastily gathered all he would need to paint the portrait of the woman he had just seen.

How beautiful she was. How rare. How... not of this earth! For she had an almost futuristic look about her. One of which could place her to another century altogether.

He smiled, caught in a feverish state of euphoria, nearly running to the office to begin his painting.

Once inside, he slammed the door behind him, the sound reverberating through the room. Then, he looked up at the lavish picture – the one he was about to paint over.

Looking down on him, unceremoniously so, was an attractive woman whose origins he knew nothing of.

The sable blackness of her eyes stared at him with pride, whilst her full vermillion lips faintly smiled. Burnished copper hair was styled and tucked neatly beneath a large cavalier-style hat enhanced with ostrich plumes of black, red, and blue. Adorning the upsweep of the brim was a large, noble silver brooch.

Holding the lady firmly within its possession, the large, decadent baroque oval-shaped frame – gilded in 22k gold – rested elegantly upon the chimney breast.

How his father, perhaps even his mother – would frown if, for one single, solitary moment, they could guess what he was about to do.

He smiled devilishly as he laid his first, rabid strokes of colour over the painting.

How freeing, how marvellous it felt.

For a few hours he painted intently when a light knock sounded beyond the other side of the door.

"Come in, Mrs March," he said, recognising her knock.

As Mrs March entered the room, the smile she boasted, briskly abandoned her face. "Why, sir! Whatever are you doing?! That's a family heirloom!" she spat out, completely flabbergasted.

"I've no idea who these people are," he replied whilst upholding full concentration of his almost frenzied sweeps of paint.

"They're your family!"

"I care nothing for these dusty old relics."

"Dusty?!" she replied with mortification.

"I do beg your pardon." He looked away from his work for a short while and cast her an apologetic look.

Then returning to his art began once again. "But relics they are, nonetheless… I have no concerns for these people that hang about the walls unnoticed by all who pass them by. I know nothing of them, and I've never met them. They stare out from the walls ignored with barren expressions displayed upon their faces, whilst we go about our lives paying no heed to them. We walk about the house giving them not a moments glance. It's as though they're not there.

They're of no consequence to me.

My only interest is my sanity, and right now, right at this very moment, my dear Mrs March, I am the sanest, *and* happiest I have felt for some time."

"But, Master Roman sir. That portrait is hundreds of years old," she protested.

"The 17th century, at least," he replied with an impish look of amusement. "What was it you wanted of me?"

"Oh, yes. I'd forgotten completely, what with the shock of…" She halted mid-sentence whilst looking sternly at the painting. "Dinner is ready to be served, sir."

He put down his paintbrush and easel and wiped his hands clean of paint on a rag that had the full spectrum of colours dried within it from years of use. "I didn't realise the time. Forgive me. Would you consider it a terrible inconvenience if I were to ask you to place my dinner on a tray for me? You see, I'm absorbed in my work and would pain me to leave it, even for dinner." He smiled graciously at her.

"Of course, sir. It's no inconvenience."

"Thank you, Mrs March. That's most agreeable of you."

"Will that be all, sir?"

"Would you be so kind as to attend to Ferret's needs for the remainder of the evening?"

"By all means. Mr March and I love the company of Ferret," she smiled. "Though when he gets himself before the fire, he steals all the heat," she laughed.

"One of the many advantages of living a dog's life," he smiled. "Thank you, Mrs March, that will be all." He bowed in acceptance of her curtsey and subsequent leaving of the room. Then once again, picked up his brush and easel and proceeded with his painting.

The days passed in a blur as he worked ceaselessly, tirelessly on his portrait of the woman he longed to see again.

Mrs March journeyed to and fro with a successional lunch, afternoon tea, dinner, and supper trays.

Now and again a bark from Ferret would break through his curtain of captivation.

On the evening of the third day, his masterpiece was finally complete. He stood back from his work with a look of admiration about him.

He had captured her just as a camera would – mid-turn with a look of alarm graced upon her unique face. She was as he had seen her, just before she had vanished.

He had used tones of flaxen and white for the hair, for the eyes a variety of grey. The insipid colours purposely used rent her like a being caught existing simultaneously and fleetingly between two corresponding worlds.

Perhaps she was?

A frisson of excitement rippled through his body. He was in comprehendible awe of her.

For several moments now, Ferret had been outside, barking incessantly at the office window, his huge head swaying from side to side in the strangest manner.

Yet through it all, his Master remained oblivious, unmoved by the commotion. He looked almost statuesque – silent, still – his only seduction the painting before him.

But as Roman, in a dazed state, finally turned his gaze toward the shifting movement at the window, his reverie began to thin. And then, Ferret's head-splitting, ear-piercing bark tore through – strident, forceful, crashing against the silence in wild, relentless waves.

"What is it, Ferret?!" he shouted, indignation flaring at having been so abruptly torn from his thoughts.

And Now, with his Master's attention, Ferret planted his huge paws on the windowsill, each fevered bark leaving a fresh smear of saliva upon the glass.

"Ferret! What in damnation is the matter with you?!" he bellowed, striding toward the window.

With an infuriated whoosh, he flung it open. But as he reached out to soothe Ferret, his fingers met something unseen – warm, silken, and cat-like in its presence.

Then, turning wildly away, Ferret ran as if in pursuit of something.

Roman stared aghast as Ferret vanished into the innards of the cold, obsidian night, swallowed by the unsympathetic fog.

"Ferret! Ferret!" he called, his voice cutting through the stillness. "Ferret!!"

But the only sound that reached his ears was deep, guttural snarling, punctuated by the brutal clash of gnashing teeth.

As he fled the office, exasperated, racing down the corridor, a cacophony of filtered voices bellowed after him:

"Here comes a candle to light you to bed, and here comes a chopper to chop off your head! Chip chop, chip chop…"

He burst into the vacuum of fog, but the final words still found him:

" …The last man is dead!!"

Howling screams and shrieks of laughter followed, echoing in the thick murk. The word 'dead' seemed to coil through the fog, creeping, stalking – until, like him, it faltered, hesitating in the suffocating stillness.

"Ferret?!" he thundered out, unconcerned as to the perplexing voices that briefly haunted him, *or* the odd feeling on his hands before he had opened the window – as though he had pushed something out of it.

And as if in answer to his Master's command, Roman could hear Ferret's sudden ferocious barks thundering from his lungs and out through his monstrous mouth.

As Roman advanced toward the chilling growls, the fog momentarily shifted, revealing a definite frame of black – motionless before the pond.

At its base stood Ferret, rigid, muscles coiled with tension. His ears were pinned back, his hackles raised in a bristling ridge along his spine. His tail stood stiff and high, vibrating with restrained fury.

Roman knew – whatever that looming figure was, it was mere moments from being attacked. And savagely so.

"Ferret! No!!" he commanded as he ran toward him.

As the fog shifted once more, dim streaks of moonlight briefly revealed the pale pallor of a face – twisted in a contortion of terror.

And as she sang – a lullaby – 'Hush, Little Baby' – Ferret lunged, his massive paws pressing forcefully against her shoulders.

The last thing Roman Lyons saw before the fog swallowed him, masking his vision once more, was the woman falling backward into the pond – her arms crossed protectively over her chest.

For the briefest moment, he caught the shimmer of tears, the eerie lustre of her terror-stricken grey eyes – locked onto his, pleading.

Then, as silence settled and the ghostly weight of fog fell like a shroud, the last thing Roman Lyons heard was the incalculable sound of cracking and splintering – echoing murderously as the mountains of fog enwreathed him.

Part Three

The End of the Beginning

Chapter 22

Several weeks had passed since the sudden and inexplicable disappearance of Kathryn White and her beloved little cat, Ninkip. Lyon House was empty once again – some believed it should stay that way – indefinitely, that the house decreed it.

Since Halloween night, an uncanny lull had settled over Lyon House.

The fog that once smothered it had lifted, vanishing entirely to reveal the night skies of deep blue-black, where the moon and stars shone with unfiltered brilliance.

And in the days that followed, the sun burned pure and bright once more, suspended in a perfect, vibrant blue sky, lavishly patterned with decadent swathes of cloud, white as porcelain.

As Mrs Carter strolled in solemn silence through the halls, corridors, and rooms of Lyon House, it was bittersweet to know she would be the last living soul to grace its presence.

For today, the house was to be closed forever.

How sad, how dismal it would soon appear – its windows and doors stripped away, replaced only by blank, soulless boards.

Though she could understand Anna's actions, she could not bring herself to agree with them. And Kathryn, dearest Kathryn, would never approve of Lyon House being subjected to such treatment. Oh, how her heart would surely bleed.

Out of the blue, she had received a formal letter from Anna's solicitor, instructing her to close the house.

The precise words read:

'...To board up all windows and doors. My client wishes for no one to assume residence in Lyon House – ever. Her intent is clear: no one shall suffer the same fate as her much-loved sister, Kathryn. Thus, it shall remain in the ownership of the White family, untouched, perpetually.'

Mrs Carter's fingers had trembled slightly as she read the letter. How decisively it had been written – how coldly final.

The letter had gone on to state that she was to personally oversee the project.

The weight of it pressed down on her, heavier than she could bear.

Was Anna aware of what she was truly asking? To witness the slow suffocation of Lyon House, to silence its walls, to erase its history with blank, soulless boards? To be the one to close its doors forever? And Kathryn – dearest Kathryn – how she had once breathed life into these halls, her laughter and happiness spun into the very fabric of its being. The way Lyon House had cradled her like something sacred.

Mrs Carter exhaled, slow and measured.

The very walls seemed to breathe around her, holding onto their final hours.

But it was no use – she could still feel her, still hear her – the whisper of Kathryn's voice lingered in the quiet. And now, she was expected to close it forever, to lock away Kathryn's essence among growing dust and decay. The thought was unbearable.

She had tried countless times to contact Anna to reason with her. But all her telephone calls and messages continued to be ignored and unanswered.

And now, drilling and hammering reverberated morosely through the house as its daylight was gradually stolen. She had felt indebted to Mr Woodsman for leaving her a candle – this morning he had disconnected all the electrical and numerous other systems the house depended upon to give it life.

He placed Kathryn's newly restored painting by Mr Hardaker on the fire mantlepiece in the drawing room, as she specified. She believed that Kathryn would have wanted it there, so she instructed Mr Woodsman to do the same.

As she walked past the mural of Roman Lyons in the staircase hall, she stopped and held the candle's light to his face.

Such a supremely handsome man, she thought.

"I think Kathryn had a little crush on you, you know." Mrs Carter smiled, a reflective glint in her eyes. "That poor girl!"

She reached for a handkerchief in her pocket and dabbed her emotion-filled eyes dry.

"You know, she once asked me if you lived happily ever after. I didn't know then, but I do now. She would've been thrilled to learn that you did, indeed, go on to live a long, full, and extraordinarily happy life.

If my research serves me correctly, you met and married your soulmate, with whom you had one child. And oh, Mr Lyons – how I wish Kathryn could've known, for it feels almost fated that she lived here. Your wife's name, too, was Kathryn. And your daughter – Anna! She would've been awestruck! For she adored this house, you know, and all to do with it."

She hesitated, exhaling slowly. "It's such a shame she's gone. The worst thing is not knowing where... nor what has become of her and little Ninkip."

Her gaze flitted over the portrait, lingering.

"She used to stand right here, staring up at you, imagining – wondering what life had been like behind these walls in your time. Had she known what I know now, she would've felt even more tethered to this place. She would have clung to it with everything she had."

A sudden hush settled over the room, thick and waiting.

Lyon House listened.

The wooden floorboards beneath Mrs Carter's feet groaned softly, as though shifting under the weight of memory.

A faint stirring – a breath that wasn't hers – moved through the still air, unsettling the candle's flame.

She stilled.

The house exhaled. A hush of history settling into place.

She knew that if Kathryn were alive, no force on this earth could have torn her from Lyon House – such was her love, her connection to it. And so, there was only one conclusion: Kathryn was no longer of this world.

Such a beautiful girl... And Ninkip – poor, sweet, innocent little Ninkip! What in *God's* name had become of her?!

She could only hope, with every aching piece of her heart, that wherever they were, they were together.

She dried her eyes once more and followed the candle's glow into the drawing room. As she stepped inside, the last residue of daylight was choked – a board secured over the one remaining windowpane, sealing the house's fate.

Now, all was silent. All was dark.

Only her one solitary flame remained, flickering naked and bare through the oppressive curtain of obscurity.

She made her way to the fireplace and looked up at the grandly sized painting. Mr Woodsman had left the scrupulous packaging intact, leaning it safely against the wall.

For a moment, she hesitated. Should she leave it be? Was it truly her place to lay eyes upon it, when the privilege – the pleasure – should, of course, belong to Kathryn alone?

Her fingers twitched at her side, drawn toward the wrapping. Just a glimpse – surely, just a glimpse would not hurt. But the thought of peeling back even the slightest corner felt like a betrayal, like pulling apart the fragile threads of a story that was not hers to finish.

And in some small way, she hoped that by leaving the painting untouched, a spark of hope might remain. A hope that Kathryn would one day return, that *she* would be the one to lift the cover, to see with her own eyes what had always belonged to her.

Having resolved that her decision was the right one, she left the drawing room, pulling the door shut behind her. But barely had it clicked into place when a sound – a deep, shifting disturbance – rippled through the silence, beckoning her back.

Something about it – low, deliberate, pressing – caught in her chest like an unspoken word. Without thinking, she turned, hand falling to the handle, and stepped inside once more.

There, on the floor before the fireplace, lay the painting, having slipped from the mantlepiece. The packaging, once pristine, was now torn – a small portion of the paper peeled away, revealing the backing beneath.

And there, in the lower right-hand corner, was a short, handwritten note, presumably left by the artist:

'The Lyons – Mr. and Mrs. Roman and Kathryn Lyons of Lyon House, 1913.'

She placed her candle onto the mantlepiece and gradually slid, shunted, lifted, and pirouetted the painting up and around, until finally leaning it against the wall beside the fireplace.

"Forgive me Kathryn dear," she said tenderly and curiously as she lightly tore through the packaging.

When the painting was peeled of its covering, she engaged her candle and radiated its clarity upon its subject.

The portrait depicted Roman Lyons standing tall, dressed in the height of his era's refinement – as expected of a man of his notability. Beside him, to his left, sat a sleek, grey dog – a majestic Great Dane – its posture dignified, its gaze fixed upon the lady whose long, white-gloved hand Roman held with such gentleness.

She sat gracefully in a chair, looking up at him; their eyes locked in adoration. Oh, how they smiled – how happiness lived in the very lines of their faces. Such contentedness. Such *completion*.

She was lavishly dressed in a loose, short-sleeved elephant-grey evening gown, adorned with intricate lace and delicate beadwork. Its fabric cascaded to the floor in long, overlapping sensual swathes.

On her shoulder, just to the right of the open square neckline, sat the most striking brooch she had ever seen – diamond-shaped, adorned with a constellation of smaller diamonds surrounding a magnificent emerald. Below it, plunging with effortless grace, hung another emerald, pear-shaped and gleaming. Both gems shimmered with a vibrant blue-green hue.

Her dark blonde hair was piled atop her head in undulating wave-like curls, crowned by a bandeau of rhinestones. And nestled peacefully on her lap was a beautiful grey kitten, its ears remarkably large – second only, of course, to little Ninkip.

Mrs Carter's mouth parted slightly in bewilderment. Her breath caught – just for a moment as she stared up at the portrait. The candle's flame flickered, sending shadows dancing along the edges of the frame.

Her breath hitched as the truth settled. "Ninkip? ...Kathryn? ...Dear?" Her voice trembled, thick with something she could not yet name – hope, shock, perhaps even awe.

She pressed a hand to her chest as if to steady the swell of emotion rising within her.

A breathless laugh escaped her – a sound of sheer disbelief, edged with the fragile joy of a truth too big to grasp all at once.

"*Oh, my dear...*"

Her lips curled into a smile, her fingers tightening slightly around the handkerchief at her side as tears sprang from her eyes. She felt a gentle and comforting realisation, like a loving embrace.

Tears warmed her cheeks, spilling freely now, unstoppable.

Kathryn and Ninkip were not lost to tragedy, nor stolen away into the void of the unknown. *They were alive, together* – just somewhere else, *somewhen* else. A different time, yet still *here* in a way that mattered.

She wiped her damp face hastily, looking back at the portrait, at Roman, at the undeniable proof before her. The past had folded to the future. *Kathryn had found him. They had found each other.*

She had once read of a Gaelic belief in the existence of 'Thin Places' – locations where the laws of time and space are momentarily suspended, particularly during October, with the 31st being the most potent. It was said that on such days, past, present, and future could coexist in a synchronous reality. She had spoken of it with great delight to Kathryn during the Halloween party, her voice bright with belief:

"It is said that on Halloween, the veil between the earth and the spirit world is at its thinnest – sometimes lifting, if only for a moment, allowing the two realms to merge. Therefore allowing 'Time Which Is No Time' to take place. The Celts call it 'a precarious and spectacular time of union'.

Perhaps Lyon House is built upon one of those such places?"

She glanced toward the shadowed hallway beyond, a hush settling once more.

The candle flickered – not from a breeze, but something subtler, *older*. As though the house had heard her thoughts... and quietly agreed.

And for that, Mrs Carter knew – against all logic, against everything the world would deem possible – that love had, indeed, found a way.

Lyon House is not cursed.

Lyon House is merely misunderstood.

Mr Hardaker was right. The woman in the painting *is* Kathryn White.

For when fate decrees two souls are meant to be together, the bounds of time, space, law, and understanding shall be cut, bent, and shaped to ensure their union – because they were always intended to be one.

True love will always prevail.

It will always, *always* find a way.

'The Lyons' Book Soundtrack

The Wedding Dance Waltz – Titanic Orchestra
Granada – Titanic Orchestra
On the Beautiful Blue Danube – Titanic Orchestra
Merry Widow Waltz – Titanic Orchestra
Chambre Separee – Titanic Orchestra
Tales of the Vienna Woods – Titanic Orchestra
Wiener Blut – Titanic Orchestra
Sphinx – Titanic Orchestra
Lied Ohne Worte – Titanic Orchestra
Emperor Waltz – Titanic Orchestra
Songe d'Automne – Titanic Orchestra
Moonlight Sonata – Ludwig van Beethoven
Nature Boy – Nat King Cole

Listen and enjoy for free on my YOUTUBE channel POETRY IN MOTION:
(link can be found via my website – kaysnow.co.uk on 'SOCIAL MEDIA LINKS')

About the Author

I was born in the quaint town of Bingley, England. History enthusiasts might recognise it as 'The Throstles Nest of Old England,' a name mentioned in the formidable Domesday Book.

Bingley is also just a short distance from Haworth, the beloved home of the Brontë sisters. My preferred among them is Charlotte, the brilliant author of *Jane Eyre* – one of my all-time favourite books. I have a passion for reading and watching anything that features dark, brooding, Gothic Victorian mansions. Many evenings, I find myself escaping into the Gothic world through books, movies, or TV series.

As a child, I dreamed of evoking emotions in others, and what better way to do that than by becoming a singer or actress? However, my innate shyness posed a challenge. Writing became the next best thing for me. Over the years, I dabbled but never took it seriously until I entered Yahoo's writing competition. This global call for writers aimed to entertain children during the 2020 spring/summer lockdown of the Covid-19 pandemic.

Despite never having written a children's story before, I embraced the challenge. My self-belief paid off, and my story, 'The Diary of Primrose Goldie Gold,' won and was featured in Yahoo's debut edition of the STOR14S 2020 podcast series, narrated by Hollywood actress Megalyn Echikunwoke.

My first book, *The Lyons*, a gothic novel, was published in 2021. My second book, *The Land Army Girls Are Here*, a WW2 comedy-drama, followed in 2023. My third book, *Deightonby Street*, a comedy-drama set in 1944 was published in 2024. This makes me a multi-genre author, writing about whatever ignites my passion at the moment. So, stay tuned for the unexpected in my next book...

kaysnow.co.uk

Also By Kay Snow:

The Land Army Girls Are Here – a WW2 comedy-drama

Feisty eighteen-year-old Yorkshire girl April Thornton has decided to join the Women's Land Army. Feeling proud and elated, but against her parents' wishes, she leaves home in search of pastures new to work on the land, doing her bit for King and country during WW2 in 1944.

For outspoken and vivacious April, nothing less than a drama or two is classed as a boring and uneventful day, so...

Fields ploughed, harvests reaped and livestock tended – check. Dashed hopes, disasters and disappointments – check. Sex mad G.I.s, abusive farmers and bullies dealt with – check. Fun, hysterics and uproar had – an *almighty* check!

If you're a fan of Jenny Holmes and Shirley Mann novels, TV series *Land Girls* and the movie *The Land Girls*, then you'll love *The Land Army Girls Are Here*!

Deightonby Street – a comedy-drama set in 1944

Thurnscoe, South Yorkshire, England.

The pit village awakens with the dawn – a tapestry of terraced houses, each brick etched with stories of endurance. The war may scar the landscape, but it cannot extinguish the spirit of this down-to-earth working-class community, forged in coal and grit. The war casts its shadow, yet life persists.

On Deightonby Street three friends in their thirties navigate the highs and lows of life, love, conflicts, neighbours, children, and the formidable Doris Price.

Will happily married Lucy Hobson give in to her mutual passionate feelings for her daughter's charming G.I. friend, Paul?

Will Meg Emmett find the courage to stand up to her abusive husband and open her heart to new love?

Will handsome Eddie Calpin's unwavering romantic pursuit of the unimpressed Dot Moore finally pay off? Will she give in to her hidden desires?

As the sun dips behind slag heaps, the houses hold their secrets – the laughter, the grief, the unwavering hope.

ARC REVIEWS:

"Calling all Coronation Street, Emmerdale, Mount Pleasant and EastEnders fans – check out Deightonby Street. You'll LOVE it."

"Hilarious, a scream, a hoot, a joy – brilliant read."

"This should be on Netflix. Where for art thou?!"

"So, Coronation Street and Emmerdale got together and made a baby – Deightonby Street."

"I love Deightonby Street!"

Manufactured by Amazon.ca
Bolton, ON